Praise for

"Excellent and peculiar . . . Ausubel's imagination . . . wants to offer consolation for how ghastly things can get, a type of healing that only reading can provide. All eleven of these stories are deeply involving."   —*The New York Times Book Review*

"Anxious, whimsical, and deeply felt, Ausubel's stories weave a remarkable and beautiful tapestry of emotion. . . . Ausubel's signature ability to create atmosphere is in full force throughout *Awayland*, and the surreal or discomfiting moods sometimes wrapped around the stories are fitting for characters moving away from their comfort zones. By also touching upon social and political issues, she adds a new layer to her work that invites readers to move away from their comfort zones as well."   —*Los Angeles Review of Books*

"A stunning assemblage of quasi-magical yet bewilderingly plausible tales . . . Every story here pretty much astounds for its daring, visionary scope and compassion."   —*San Francisco Chronicle*

"[Ausubel] imbues every one of her offbeat yarns . . . with weirdness and warmth."   —*O, The Oprah Magazine*

"[A] collection of funny, endearing short stories . . . Each tale looks to the future in its own particular, touching way."

—*Harper's Bazaar*

"A tenderly imagined story collection, one that traverses small towns and tropical islands, all the while revealing truths about parenthood, love, and growing up that you didn't know you needed to hear, but are so immensely glad you did."   —*Southern Living*

"Fans of [Ramona Ausubel] and new readers alike will discover something to enjoy in *Awayland*. . . . An eclectic, humorous mix."

—*Real Simple*

"Few story collections in recent memory have been as simultaneously funny, sad, and peculiar as Ramona Ausubel's breathtaking *Awayland*. . . . Playful yet affecting, *Awayland* is the vibrant work of a gifted storyteller." —*Shelf Awareness*

"With touches of magic and fabulism, this is Ausubel at her finest." —*Read It Forward*

"[Ausubel's] writing is acrobatic: colorful, flexible, and inventive. . . . Formally and thematically, this creative collection will be a rewarding expedition for both veteran short story readers and newcomers to the genre." —*The Riveter*

"Ramona Ausubel's second short-story collection continues to prove her a surprising, funny, and deft fabulist." —*B&N Reads*

"Told in prose at once spare and image laden, the stories are illuminating and memorable, with plots unfolding like exotic flowers, calm yet bizarre." —*Library Journal* (starred review)

"Everyday worries about pregnancy, mortality, and parents are given fantastical treatment in these playful stories. . . . Ausubel's best stories have an affecting vulnerability; fans of Kelly Link, Karen Russell, and Miranda July will want to give this a look." —*Publishers Weekly*

"Eleven stories laced with humorous developments, mythic tendencies, and magical realist premises. Ausubel is, at heart, a fabulist, and the current collection puts this impulse in the forefront." —*Kirkus Reviews*

"In vivid, precisely fashioned language, Ausubel spans the globe, from the tropics to the Arctic, in these eleven stories. . . . Vibrant stories that expand horizons and minds." —*Booklist*

Awayland

(*Stories*)

RAMONA AUSUBEL

RIVERHEAD BOOKS

New York

RIVERHEAD BOOKS
An imprint of Penguin Random House LLC
penguinrandomhouse.com

The following stories have been previously published: "You Can Find Love Now"
(*The New Yorker*); "Fresh Water from the Sea" (*Ploughshares*); "Club Zeus"
(*Tin House*); "Heaven" (*Bullett*); "The Animal Mummies Wish to Thank the Following"
(*The Paris Review*); "Do Not Save the Ferocious, Save the Tender" (*Oxford American*).

The Library of Congress has catalogued the Riverhead hardcover edition as follows:

Names: Ausubel, Ramona, author.
Title: Awayland : stories / Ramona Ausubel.
Description: New York : Riverhead Books, 2018.
Identifiers: LCCN 2017021143 (print) | LCCN 2017025642 (ebook) |
ISBN 9780698410862 (eBook) | ISBN 9781594634901 (hardcover)
Classification: LCC PS3601.U868 (ebook) | LCC PS3601.U868 A6 2018 (print) |
DDC 813/.6—dc23
LC record available at https://lccn.loc.gov/2017021143
p.   cm.

First Riverhead hardcover edition: March 2018
First Riverhead trade paperback edition: March 2019
Riverhead trade paperback ISBN: 9781594634918

Printed in the United States of America
1 3 5 7 9 10 8 6 4 2

Book design by Gretchen Achilles

For my parents

Contents

Bay of Hungers

The Cape of Persistent Hope

The Lonesome Flats

The Dream Isles

Bay of
Hungers

You Can Find
Love Now

You are lonely, but you don't have to be. You have so many great qualities! Just think of all the single ladies out there who are waiting to hear from you. Whether you are looking for lasting love or just a little fun, this is the only guide to online dating you'll ever need. Within the hour, you'll be on your way to eternal happiness!

Let's get started. When creating your username keep in mind that it should be concise and easy to remember. Make it personal. If you're a dancer, maybe try hipdancer21.

Find me at cyclops15. Cyclops 1 through 14 were taken.

Now choose a tagline that will attract the woman you want. Secret: do what no one else is doing.

I'm eight feet tall and I have one giant eye.

What are your interests? Be honest but enticing.

I hand-sew my own shoes using a needle made from the fang of a wolf. I sleep hot. I want nothing more than a sheet on my bed, even in winter, even in a cave.

Know who your target is. Where does she live? What does she look like? What hobbies does she have?

I like fat girls, old girls, tall girls, tired girls. Girls who lack adequate clothing, girls whose best idea for getting my attention is to send a photo of themselves holding suggestive Popsicles, their fists covered in red melt. Girls in wheelchairs, girls who work professionally at the Renaissance Faire.

You could choose other men: men who like to think

about feet, men who have thick back hair, men whose greatest pride is the time they flew to a nearby nation and tried to deplete its stores of alcohol and slept on the beach one night—wasn't that so fun?—and when they woke up everything had been stolen or lost and they had to walk back to the pastel-yellow hotel naked in the early heat of another day in paradise. Everyone has had good times. Everyone has a picture of himself in front of a pinkening sunset with a glass of white wine. Choose them if you want to. Choose me if you want someone to hold you above his head in the moonlight, bite your wrist until the first rust comes out.

Tell the ladies a little more about yourself! What's your own unique story?

The first generation of Cyclopes were forgers. The next generation, my generation, was a band of thuggish shepherds living in the grasslands of Sicily. We trapped so-called heroes in our caves, we bit into the warm butter of a human leg, but the only one who got famous for it was my brother. We still live under volcanoes, hacking at iron, trying to revive the old tradition. I left home—too hot, too old—and live in Washington state. I like the fog,

I like the rain. My volcano is more famous than any of my brothers' volcanoes. I never hear from them. They're not on email.

I teach online English classes, not to get paid but because I like to feel smarter than someone else. I teach all the classic books, except *The Odyssey*.

My photos are taken in profile. Maybe there's time to get braver, to embrace my own unique beauty. I subscribe to the magazines that tell me we are all beautiful, if only we can learn to tap into our potential; I am me and no one else is me, and that is a miracle. I am a miracle.

The downside: my mother has been dead for some hundreds of years, so you'll never meet her. The upside: my father is the god of the sea, so we can guarantee good weather on our honeymoon cruise. He's shitty at love, my dad. He smells like an overcleaned wound, and he won't quit working. Every day and every night somewhere in one of the world's oceans my father is striking the surface of the abyss with swords of fire.

Do you smoke? Do you drink? How often do you exercise? Do you support charities that help animals? With an unexpected bonus would you (a) donate to a cause you really believe in? (b) save half and spend the rest? (c) celebrate with your friends and margaritas?

If you want me to set a trap, I'll set a trap. A first date picking blueberries in the whitest, cleanest sunlight, tin pails. I'll bring sandwiches and chilled Chardonnay and tell you that we are already the good people we wanted to become. Maybe you'll be generous and keep up the conversation all afternoon. Prettykaren98 was generous. Prettykaren98 looked into my eye when we chatted online and laughed at my jokes. But she never answered my messages after our date even though her status was still marked Single.

Don't mention your previous relationship history! Leave your emotional baggage packed and in the closet. You are on the market because you are awesome!

Sorry. Let's try that again. My actual perfect day? Descending belowground early, full of milk and blood and meat, to forge iron. There is no such thing as day or night in the volcano, and any sense of time comes from watching the metal change shape. From ore to spear. From ore to trident. From ore to thunderbolt. If I am strong that day, the mountains will shake with the strike of my hammer, the heat of my flame.

I can't ski. I should be better at basketball than I am. I don't eat vegetables. But my eye is blue, and it's pale and it's beautiful.

My vision is good, though not great, but understand this: I will never again visit an ophthalmologist or an optometrist or anyone else who claims to be an expert of my organ. I do not fit in the chair, and I wish I could forget lying on my back on the floor of that darkened room while a small man climbed onto my chest with that sharp point of light. I'm not sorry for what I did to him. Now he can see for himself what it's like to have one eye.

You have almost finished creating a magnetic online-dating profile that will attract more women than you ever thought possible! What else do you want the ladies to know? Remember: be yourself!

I do remember the old feeling sometimes. A maiden washes up on my island, tailed or otherwise. The cave is sweating and there are mineral stalks growing from the ceiling. I have no idea what time it is, ever. All my wrist and ankle shackles are homemade, struck from iron I myself dug from the earth. The maidens were not as beautiful as the stories tell you—their hair was salt-stringy and their faces were pruned. Too long in seawater can unmake any loveliness. Yet I meant to love them. I meant to tend to their wounds. When I pounded the shackles with my hammer, the person I imagined chaining was my father. I imagined slipping the cuffs around his watery arms. Not to hurt him, but to keep him. But my father never offered himself up on my rocky beach. I'd see his big hand out there sometimes, swilling the surface of the sea, but he never came close. Maybe he was the one who threw the maidens to me, his dear son, his wifeless boy, wanting an heir.

I will not shackle your slender wrists to the cold walls or gnaw your nails down to the quick with my remaining teeth. I will not leave you hungry while I eat a roast goat at your feet. I've dealt with those issues. Imagine the inverse: I have the softest mattress in the world, made of the combed fur of fawns; choose me and you'll be choosing warm oil on your hands and cold water in your glass, meat on your plate from a lamb that suckled on my pinkie when it was first born.

If I came to your house tonight, where would I find you? The living room? The kitchen? Waiting at the door? I'll call you Aphrodite and smell the sea in your hair and

Fresh Water from the Sea

The woman was weeks away from the end. Maybe even days away.

The phone calls at first were difficult to understand. "You shouldn't worry about this, but I'm getting thinner," she said to her daughter, but instead of the note of excitement the girl expected, the woman sounded lost. "There's less of me." The girl imagined an old woman, her spine collapsing in on itself, giving in to gravity.

"Shrinking?" she asked.

"I'm losing myself," the mother tried. The girl thought of her mother sitting on the floor of her apartment, the expensive rug covered in the puzzle pieces of her body. "It's not like that," the woman had explained. "It's like I'm vanishing. Like I am a thick fog, burning off."

The girl flew across the country: LAX, JFK, then across the Atlantic, across the Mediterranean to Beirut. The mother answered the door. She was slightly wispy. Where she had once been a precise oil painting, now she was a watercolor. "It's good of you to come." She looked the girl up and down and the girl knew her mother was disappointed to see that the girl still looked the way she always had. "Any boyfriends?"

"No boyfriends." The girl tried to smile, tried to keep the old joke alive.

Reluctantly, the woman hugged her and the girl thought, *My goodness, has she always had all of those bones?*

The mother sat down on the couch in front of the huge windows, looking out at the city and the sea beyond. She patted the spot next to her. "You see it, too, right?" She put her palm up. The girl nodded. It was just the very edges of her mother that were foggy. The girl reached out and held her mother's hand, which felt like it was coated in sea foam. "Good. I'm not going crazy," the woman said.

They sat there quietly. For two days, since her mother had first called, the girl had tried to imagine what she would look like. She had tried to prepare herself for the worst. The words "My mother is vanishing" had been like a loose piece of metal rattling around the cage of her brain. She had felt a little bit of electricity shoot through her system, a jig of hopefulness. *Maybe we will actually say something real to each other,* she thought. Now, she was wordless. "It's good to see you," the girl said. She stood at the edge, just where she always had.

From her suitcase she removed a jar of peanut butter, a box of cereal bars, oatmeal, pinto beans and a loaf of whole wheat bread. "A little bit of America."

The girl thought she could see a wisp of her mother disappear, right then. "I'm sure it's just . . . something," she said, trying to stop it. The mother, misty, smiled at her daughter.

Out the window, they could see the tops of buildings, the air-conditioning units and heating tubes and collections of wires. The minaret from the mosque craned its neck. Below, café people were sitting with their legs crossed at the ankle and their faces up to the sun. This part of the city had been crumbled in the last war and was built back all at once, the center of the city turned into an overcheerful mall. Plaza and clock tower, cobbled streets radiating out with shops.

"It looks just like California," the girl said. She had taken a class on the American Dream in which the students wrote papers about the exporting of culture.

"At least it's intact," her mother said. She gestured to the other window through which a big hotel stood, its walls yawning with holes, the railings on the balconies mangled. It was so quiet, that bombed-out hotel. *How strange,* the girl thought, *that only the visual evidence of a war is recorded.*

Beyond the city, the sea was endless.

The rest of the afternoon, the girl and her mother did what people do: went on in spite of what had changed. They chatted a circle around the outskirts of their lives, they ate something when they got hungry. By the time they went to bed, the woman's blurry edges had become just another fact of the world, a stray cat that, once let in, had made itself at home.

IN THE MORNING, the girl and her mother packed up for the doctor's appointment, put on decent-looking clothes. The girl did not say that her mother was a little hazier than she had been the day before. She did not say that, when she came close to her mother, the temperature changed, as if the woman was her own weather system.

The doctor refused to look the mother in the eye or smile, as if doing so would break his calm. He asked a lot of questions that seemed like a way of avoiding what else he had to say. He wanted to know whether she'd been sleeping, and how about the chills, had she had any? And whether her snot, which she reported having a little of, was green or yellow.

"Clear," she told him.

He said, "That's great," with conviction that surprised even him. "I mean," he fumbled, "that's good."

The girl raised her eyebrows and nodded. "Her eyes are fine, too," she said, "and everything's shipshape with her toenails."

"We'll run some blood tests," he said, and they all knew that he meant *This is a new way to get there, but the end will be the same.* The girl stood up and left the room. She went into the sterile-smelling bathroom and sat down on the toilet and kicked the wall once, hard. It clanked. There was a rubber mark on the wall from the black sole of her sneaker. She opened the little window where the pee samples were supposed to go. It was empty at the moment. She could see, through plastic curtains, technicians adjusting dials on the machines. They appeared as if underwater, breathing miraculously, collecting and testing out the life around them. Determining the lengths of time everyone had left on this alien land. She wanted to ask for forgiveness or clemency. Her mother hardly knew her at all, and she suspected the reverse was also true. She had always expected some midlife understanding, a trip to India in which they wore a lot of loose white clothing, finally revealed their true selves, said all those unsayables. On one of the little paper pee cups, in the marker that was meant to be used to write your name on the sample, the girl scrawled: *Give us more time, please. As much as you can spare.*

ON THE SECOND DAY, the girl left her mother asleep on the couch in the sun and went walking. Ahead of her, the sea was pane-smooth, and in a square looking out at it, a statue of an angel shot full of holes. The girl thought of the Mediterranean, the mythic voyages, the wars. It seemed strange that it was also just a place—dirt and water and wind. A taxi driver swerved and honked at an old woman crossing the road and then stopped short to buy a newspaper from a child. The girl remembered the city, but not well. She had visited her grandparents when they were alive, eaten sugar-syrup pastries in the sun, driven into the mountains and looked out at the sea. "The cliffs will eventually erode," her grandfather had said, gesturing. "See how the water keeps tugging at them?" There was an underground river of desperation in his voice. This country was not big enough to lose any more ground.

The girl watched boys jump from the sea wall into the deep blue. Families had chairs set up along the boardwalk, lunches, hookahs, children with candy-stuck faces. They were alive and together and God, whichever god was theirs, had shaken this day out like a crisp sheet for them to lie down on.

The girl sat on a bench and called her sister who was planning, always planning, to worry about someone besides herself. "It really is like she's fading away," the girl said over the thousands and thousands of miles. It felt strange to say it, and she looked around to see if anyone had overheard her. The girl waited to be carted off, a crazy daughter.

"I just wish I was there," the sister told her.

"You can be. There are airplanes."

"God," she kept sighing, "give Mom a big kiss for me."

"How is Dad handling it?"

"Handling it? They haven't spoken in years. He's fine."

"Is this really happening?" the girl asked, but her sister had already hung up.

THE STORY, the way it had always been told, was this: When the woman was eighteen years old, the war had woken back up. Her parents sent her away with a suitcase full of gifts for the relatives in California who had agreed to take her in. "But I don't know who I am anywhere else."

The parents said, "You'll be whoever you become." On the airplane, the woman had cried until her cheeks were sore, her eyelids swollen, her lips raw. She promised herself to her country, swore she would never love anything or anyone else.

She planned to go home in a year, but her parents matched her up with the boy who lived down the street. The woman did not fall in love with him, but she married him because it was easier than not marrying him. She pinned photographs of that faraway coastline to the ceiling above her bed, stared up at the relentless blue sea while her husband breathed into her neck. Then the woman was pregnant with twin girls, a pair of anchors that would sink into the sand of their adopted city.

When the girls were young, everything in the house had come from the woman's faraway home. Olives, sweets, citrus, honey. The first thing the daughters learned to draw was the cedar tree, famous and endangered. Inside the house, the family lived in a tiny island of the woman's long-lost home. The girl and her sister were taught to be suspicious of everything else, California looming like a high-wire circus that wanted to recruit them. All their lullabies were from Lebanon, all their prayers. The mother surrounded herself with the seaside country like it was atmosphere, the only thing keeping her alive on a noxious, foreign planet. But the twins each seemed to belong to one parent: the girl was her mother's and the sister was their father's, which was to say that the sister was at home everywhere and the girl was at home nowhere.

The girl remembered sitting outside her parents' door before her father left, listening to them fight.

"I'm from the same place as you," the father had said.

"But you are not the place itself. You are not my home."

IN THE AFTERNOON of the third day, the woman and the girl sat on the bed playing two games of solitaire because neither one could remember the rules to anything else.

The cloud that was the mother had grown thinner. The air around her was dewy.

Outside the window the people, the poor war-battered and future-looking people, were just trying to enjoy a day in the sunshine. They were being good, trying hard. The girl thought about rewarding them, throwing chocolate coins or confetti down.

"Would you do something for me?" the mother asked her daughter. "I haven't shaved in days. I can't stand to touch my skin."

The girl filled up a pot with warm water and put on a pair of shorts. She took one of her mother's legs in her hands. Even without shaving cream, the mother's legs were puffs. For a moment, after each stroke, her skin looked like skin, as if all the girl needed to do was sweep the clouds away to find her. But soon, the mist gathered, and the woman was ghosty again.

"Why is this happening?" the girl asked.

"I'm sure it's my fault. Maybe I didn't eat enough leafy greens. Maybe I did something awful in a past life. I'm sure I should have loved you better."

"There are worse mothers, and they don't disappear."

"Everybody goes, somehow."

The mother watched while her daughter worked. She looked back and forth between their legs. "Your bone structure, sweetie," she told the girl, "it's very good. Even your ankles, look at how nicely they taper." She reached out and smoothed her finger over the girl's calf.

The mother was gently marking the girl. When, in some future, the girl let a man near her skin again, she knew already that the fingers she'd feel would be her mother's.

THE MOMENT THE GIRL and her sister were settled in college, the mother began to shop for an apartment back home. She was a brightened, colored-in version of herself. She sold off the furniture, gave away half her clothes, made her daughters reduce the relics of their childhood to two cardboard boxes, stored in their aunt's garage. Meanwhile, the girl set up pictures on her dorm-room desk, organized her sweaters in the drawer. She, too, felt like she was living in a new country—college was America and nowhere else. She felt like she had just stepped off a ship for the first time in her life, her body still listing.

The mother called occasionally at the beginning of fall to report the progress of settling in, news from friends, restaurants discovered. The girl would return her mother's calls when she got back to the dorm from a series of parties, just drunk enough to feel like talking. "How is your sister?" the woman asked. "Is she still with that what's-his-name?"

"I have no idea. I don't keep track."

"It's late. You should study." The girl put a foot on the floor to anchor herself. *Dear Mom,* she thought, *I'm really happy to be alone in the world. Thank you for being far away.* All her life, the mother's unhappiness had been like a magnet for the girl, pulling, pulling. There were so many new things for the girl to love, now that her mother was in the distance.

The girl could hear her new friends in the common room, microwaving something wonderfully horrible to eat. Her life was an unplanted field, and everywhere she looked, something waited to be sown.

ON THE FIRST DAY, the second day and all the other days, the girl did not call her father. She wished a terrible wish: that he had been the one to disappear. On the fourth day, the girl called her sister, knowing it wasn't a good time for her. She would be eating in a new restaurant with a new boyfriend who was probably on the verge of proposing just at the moment the sister would have spotted someone cuter in the yellow streetlight outside. She made the girl tired, the dance of her life. "How *is* she?" the sister said, her voice full of the overconcern of guilt.

"She's less and less," the girl said. The sister sighed. The girl knew she did not believe what was happening—none of them did. It seemed made-up, a story they were all pretending. The sister did not comfort the girl and the girl did not comfort her sister. "Are you sure you don't want to come? Consider ten years from now, won't you wish you'd seen her?" On the far end, the voices of many people, awake late at night, clinking their glasses.

"What? It's so loud here."

The girl whispered, "I can hardly hear you either, in all this quiet."

BY THE FIFTH DAY, the mother's skin was practically radiating light. She looked more and more like weather, like a brewing storm. Her face was hairless and glowing. Disappearing was what the mother was now doing, as if disappearing were a job. She was working hard at it, overachieving as usual.

The girl sat down close to her mother on the couch. She wanted to touch her mother. It was the same temptation she had had on every airplane flight of her life, looking out at those mounded clouds. There was a coolness to her mother, the chill of wet air. The girl felt something hard around her mother's waist. "What is this?" she asked, startled.

"A girdle," the mother said.

The girl paused and ran her hand up the perfect smoothness of the device, which did not give way. "Have you always worn this?"

"I was trying to find something to contain me. To hold me together."

"Let me do it," the girl said. "The last thing we need is a device that's meant to shrink you." The girl moved her hand up the long line of clasps, releasing. She put her arms around her mother's waist and she held hard. The woman was too weak to wriggle away. For this they both gave silent thanks.

The woman studied the street scene. "I never got around to sorting all my paperwork," she told her daughter. "I still have all my old gas bills in storage. It hardly seems fair that I should disappear yet they remain."

"Are there things I should keep?"

"I have no idea. Ask my accountant. Or maybe there's

some kind of packet available. 'What to do with your files when you vanish.'" They both laughed and then they both stopped laughing. "You should take the fashion magazine subscriptions for yourself. Give the political stuff to your sister."

"Yeah, she'll really love that." The girl imagined her sister with her nose curled up as if doing so could make her any less stupid, trying to understand even one line of an article about the wars, the elections.

Down below on the street there were clumps of people eating at tables. They had hummus and lamb flatbread and a bottle of wine. A man wore a T-shirt that said "Talk to My Agent." There was a rack of postcards standing on the sidewalk and a man and woman were taking out one at a time and laughing at them. They pointed and then they laughed. The girl imagined the cards: puppies dressed as policemen; old women, naked but for cat-eye sunglasses and martinis. The people found this funny. They could be anywhere on earth, any nationality, and the joke would still be the same.

"Tell me something about your life," the mother said.

"A professor asked me out. We had one boring date and a sloppy kiss. I got a B in the class and I was so furious."

The mother put her hand on the girl's. It was too soft.

"I love you," the girl said.

"Let's not do that."

The girl searched the room for something safe to look at. On the counter was a bowl with a fissure straight through, waiting to be glued. It was an old bowl, probably a gift from some beloved. Would she throw it in the garbage? Dead and over? The apartment was full of the souvenirs of a lived life, each one the nail holding a memory in place. The girl wondered, when they passed through her hands and did not jog a memory because neither the objects nor the places they came from belonged to her, if she would want to wrap them carefully in paper and ship them to herself in boxes. Or if she would send them to the poor because the objects were inanimate and mute and could not revive the woman who used to love them. Would some part of the girl suddenly bloom that knew what to do?

"Throw them away," the mother said, as if she was reading her daughter's mind. "We'll go through the apartment tomorrow and tag the good things, worth money or very special. You don't want to treasure some piece of art for the next fifty years only to meet me in heaven and discover that I always hated it."

———

LATE AT NIGHT the girl took the girdle into the guest bedroom where she was sleeping. She wrapped the girdle around herself and hook-and-eyed the long strand. She examined herself in the mirror. She wondered who would hold her in when she began to disperse.

The girl found her phone and scrolled through the contacts, wanting to hear a warm voice. She hit Send on her ex, and he answered with a question in his voice. In the background was the din of twentysomething fun. The girl said, "Hey," and the lonesomeness in her voice surprised her. The ex talked for a second, but she was listening to the party behind him. He had no idea how lucky he was to be in a room with a hundred other young bodies, complete bodies, everyone yelling to be heard. The girl hung up without saying good-bye and didn't answer when the boy called back. The room was sick with quiet. The girl took the girdle off and held it to her cheek, her mother's sweat and skin part of the fibers now, pressed together like praying hands.

A WEEK AFTER the girl had arrived, the woman was vapor. She was pure humidity, and the whole apartment was muggy with her. The marble in the bathroom sweated all day. Droplets of condensation fell from the ceiling. The air was heavy. The mother, what was left of her, hovered on the couch. Even her bones were faint. The girl called her sister to say that she didn't think the woman had long.

Someone knocked on the door a few minutes later. It was a pimpled adolescent boy with a huge bouquet. The girl closed the door to a crack. Her first thought was that God had sent these flowers—who else could have gotten them here so quickly? She pictured the all-powerful, trying to negotiate a bouquet without too many carnations. The card said, *Dear Mom: Wishing you the best in this hard time in your life.*

And what about your life? the girl thought. *I suppose this is not a hard time for you. Do you have a secret mother waiting to replace this one? Or maybe you don't need one because you have a dad?*

The girl looked at the almost-nothing that was her mother now. "Look what your daughter sent," she said. The mother looked back. The girl was completely visible, but that was not the same thing as being whole. Inside the girl, there were fractures, fault lines.

The girl stood by the open window, pulled a rose out

and threw it. It whirled in slow motion for a few seconds, like the hand on a clock, counting down. A man picked it up then turned upwards, shading his eyes and trying to figure out the source of the bloom. "What are you doing?" the mother asked.

"I guess I'm throwing roses," the girl said, unable to make sense of herself. The mother, barely a mist now, joined her by the window. A little whorl of her trailed behind and the girl swept her hand through it.

"Can I have one?" The woman tossed it and it felt good. "You can love as many and as much as you want. I thought I had to save my love up, that I would run out. It turns out it's the exact opposite." She paused. "When I was living in California, the only thing I could smell was this city. I would remember the plainest things, some random intersection, and feel an ache to see it. Missing home was sweeter even than being here."

The girl thought of all the leavings a person does over the course of her life. Leaving the womb, growing up and leaving home, letting go of friends, breakups with lovers, divorce, houses packed up and moved out of. She pictured abandoned, grown-out-of skins everywhere.

The girl could already feel the empty space forming

around her mother, and its gravity. She knew she would circle it for the rest of her life, orbiting that absence.

"When I walked out of the airport, when I finally came home, I thought *I never have to leave this.* All those years, all I had wanted was to be surrounded by this city, engulfed."

The mother told her daughter about the first weeks, which were all reunions with old friends, picnics by the sea, meals in which every single thing was right—the dreamed-of bread dipped in olive oil, the woman's fingers glistening. She woke in the seaside country, she slept in it. She breathed and it filled her up.

"Soon, I had seen each of my old friends once, and when I called for another date, their voices cooled. 'We're going away soon, and I have a million and one things to do,' one said. 'I'd really love to, but it's a busy time at work.' I used to be a once-every-three-years friend." The girl thought of the architecture of those lives in which there was a small room for her mother, quiet, off in the corner. The sitting rooms were filled with nearers and dearers, the gardens were at capacity, the bedrooms, certainly, were full.

As the months passed, the mother said she had continued to buy the dreamed-of bread and dip it in olive oil, but she did not close her eyes with pleasure each time anymore.

This was not bread from the faraway seaside country anymore—it was just bread, commonplace and unremarkable. The coffee was just coffee, the oranges just oranges. Every bakery had the treats she had eaten as a child; every café the tomato salad. The concentrate that she had spent her whole life brewing, the thick syrup of this place that she had lived on, had been watered down. Every single thing was the war-torn seaside country.

"How could I love every single thing?" she asked. "It used to be that I *was* my love for this place. With so much of the place, it was like I, too, was being diluted."

The girl thought of her mother, her mostly water body dropped into a deep blue pool, dispersing.

"I wandered street by street, buying things just so that I could say hello to the shopkeepers. I still felt unseen."

And the next week, she said, she was also unseeable. Just a little bit, at first. The woman kept taking her sunglasses off to clean them, to try and wipe away the fogginess. But the rest of the world was crisp. Her body alone was blurring. "Is this what dying feels like? I wondered. Does everyone have this experience at the end of their lives?"

"I'm sorry you were sent away," the girl said. The girl remembered hearing her mother crying in the other room as a child. She seemed to be drifting on an unknown sea. Every day, many times, the girl had tried to turn herself into an island on which her mother could land.

The girl threw another rose. A man picked it up, squinted up into the sky and the woman and the girl could tell that he did not see them this high. The mother and her daughter were nothing more than strange weather.

The girl asked her mother to tell her that they were both going to be all right. That they were both going to be at home wherever they were. She wanted it to be true, something the mother could know from her perch at the edge of life.

Out over the sea, the sun grew hotter. The girl remembered the water cycle: evaporation, condensation, precipitation. The mother closed her eyes. She was almost invisible now. She was just the faintest color, like the rainbows thrown by a crystal in the window. The air hung against the girl's skin, heavy. The woman was the air; the girl breathed her in. She looked around the room and could not see her mother anymore.

A storm broke over the girl, thunderheads, lightning, rain and rain and rain and rain.

Template for a Proclamation to Save the Species

Φ

Perhaps it is the shittiness of the northern Minnesota town that keeps her residents from reproducing. Theirs is not a furious protest, a political movement. It is as if their lives are so boring, so deeply muddy that it hardly even occurs to two people to couple with enough feeling to create anything other than a disappointed sigh.

The small town's mayor, Tom Anderson, reads a story about a mayor in a small Russian town, also cold and dark and relatively poor, also reproductively slow, who declared

September twelfth Family Contact Day. The Russian mayor said he had chosen the date because it was exactly nine months before Vladimir Lenin's birthday and he offered prizes—a station wagon, a refrigerator—for babies born on the same day as the Great Leader.

Tom had not meant to go into politics and hadn't even wanted to remain an American. He had spent a semester in college in Russia and gotten a taste for fish eggs and first-wave communism and had planned to stay and study literature but had to go home to the cold, flat north of his own America to take care of his aged aunt.

Tom thinks about a designated sex day. Everything around him is dreary. The economy droops. Winter is nigh. He takes solace in the fact that the whole city seems to have reached the sloppy bottom place, has sunk to the pond-scummy floor and that anything, it seems, would be an improvement. Tom begins to draft an announcement for the newspaper. He changes the name of the holiday to Love Day. He does not mention anything about communism or Russia—though some politicians seem to admire the brute force of Russia, this is a town where "socialism" is the dirtiest word and Tom does not want to navigate the narrow channel between admiration and fear—so he claims the idea as his own. Everyone will get the day off, and they will stay home, and they will screw. And the part that makes the mayor squeeze his fists in pride is the prize he will arrange: the first mother to give birth on June twelfth wins an economy car, a tiny white Ford.

The mayor's decree is published in the newspaper. Online, the comments are mocking. The mayor wonders how it is taken in Russia, what the Great Leader would think. Would he be proud? Or is he watching from death as his birthday is commemorated with a badly made refrigerator bestowed upon a disinterested mother, her unprepared husband and their howling alien of an infant? On one side of the glass, there is a dream of perfect equality, and on the other, life in exchange for a kitchen appliance. There is something Russian about this, the mayor thinks to himself, but he is American and doesn't know what it is.

Along with declaring the holiday, the mayor has a bench installed in the park, shaped like two hearts, side by side. The seat is curved to encourage couples to slide close together. He names this the Bench of Love. Teenagers immediately notice that from behind, the bench looks like two large butts.

In the newspaper, one Ruby Goebels is quoted: "I'm glad to have the day off. I have a lot of canning to do." Still, a day off is a day off. No one considers not taking advantage of it. The question is whether the people will allow their city government to dictate their sex schedule. For many, it is a humiliation, and instead husband and wife plan to sit side by side on the couch with the television blaring, drinking three fingers of whiskey at a time until someone gets hungry and opens a package of hot dogs.

For the teenagers, there is much confusion. It is in their nature not to do as they are told, yet what they have been told to do is so acutely in line with what they want. It is only when some of them point out that no one wants *them* to have babies, unmarried as they are, that they all rejoice, head to the big park after dark—thrilled to have been returned to that beloved state of disobedience—to find vaguely hidden hollows in which to fuck. Every few decades, the teenagers think, a politician might have a good idea.

MARTHA AND JEFF act as if it is a Sunday—they cook bacon for breakfast and have beer with it. Martha does their laundry, folding her husband's dozens of similarly striped T-shirts and baggy jeans and laying them in piles on the sofa. Across the street, Fat Henderson is standing naked, in profile, examining himself in the mirror. He looks pregnant. Martha cannot see his crotch, a fact she is grateful for, but she can't help but think of the sad little display it must be: a deflated prize resting on two swollen, purple pillows. Martha imagines that Fat Henderson is trying to find a way of asking his wife to take up the mayor's suggestion, despite the fact that they are beyond the age of conception.

Martha and Jeff have been married since they were both pretty. She still is; the American man has a shorter window. His mother told him each morning in high school: "Your hairline is already beginning to retreat, your eyeballs will bulge like your father's, your ears will grow and your lips will thin. You had better sign something with that girl of yours before it's too late."

Martha believes that her looks have a very specific expiration. She believes that no matter what kind of care she takes of her body, of her face, she will turn into an old lady the moment she has a child. It is like a fairy-tale curse on these midwestern plains. The short mom hair, the square shelf of a butt, the minivan: they are fate, unavoidable, and their emergence will begin as soon as sperm and egg meet.

Whether this sad progression could be thwarted is untested. No generation of women has ever avoided becoming parents. Martha's mother was a baby machine, congratulated by the church for her eleven children. For eighteen years straight, Martha's mother had a shitting baby in the house. Martha had arrived in the middle, between Paula and Matthew, the only boy. She had no special role to play, not the oldest nor the youngest, not the idolized boy. Martha was part of an assembly line. She grew up with the feeling that children must simply appear, unbidden. Who would want to make any more of them? It was as if they hatched in some dirty, neglected corner like so many baby cockroaches and the grown-ups had had no choice but to try to raise them.

MARTHA AND JEFF are pressed up against the wall in the living room on Love Day. They do not draw the shades. Martha can see a ghost of their reflection in the glass panes of a china cabinet she inherited from her grand-mother. She admires her husband's butt and her own lithe arms around his back. In the middle, Martha thinks to herself—*There it goes*. She can almost feel her calves fatten, her feet flatten and her hair turn gray. It is the exact ending of youth. Yet somehow, she is not completely sorry to see it go. She has been pretty a long time, and she is curious what the world looks like for someone who is invisible to men. What will it be like to walk down the street without getting the looks from every truck driver, every guy standing outside in the bitter cold, his own stale breath billowing out as dark and dirty as smoke?

From her position, she has a view of the whole room. Like a hologram, she sees the way it will change. The wicker bassinet will take up that corner, there will be toys all over the floor, a pile of laundry. She sees herself, and it makes her tired. When the baby comes, Martha knows, it will make her wonder whether anything else has ever been true. *You thought all that mattered?* the world will say. That old life was a set, just a painted background.

FOR THE NEXT NINE MONTHS, a small Ford will sit in front of the mayor's office adorned with a big red bow, which fades in the meager sunlight. He will look out at it every few hours and allow the warmth to fill his chest.

IN FEBRUARY, at the supermarket, Martha runs into Na-thalie, a math tutor and the wife of the high school wres-tling coach who really wants to win the car. "It's the only reason good enough to ruin this body," Nathalie says, running her hands up and down her hips and waist like they are for sale. Nathalie asks if Martha's disinterest in the competition is a carefully crafted strategy, some kind of conniving.

IN A UNIQUE FERTILITY RITUAL, the wrestling coach hangs up magazine ads of small American cars around the bed. He is already picking out accessories for the new car. He has decided that he will have a car shower on the day his wife has a baby shower so that each pink or blue bib will be met with an after-market alarm system, an expensive-looking stereo, a mountain-lemon-scent air freshener in the shape of a sexy mermaid and a set of perfectly unnecessary mud flaps, considering that the car will barely have enough clearance for a mall speed bump.

HE DOES NOT say it out loud, but Tom has complicated feelings about being in power. There is shame, of course, in the fact that he had won his election with no opponent. All the other men in town must have figured out that they could make much more money—and suffer much less scrutiny—by working in office buildings and construction sites than by serving the public. The mayor's constituents assumed he was in it for the same reasons politicians here always had been—a little money skimmed off the top to buy veal, blondes. No one begrudged him because no one believed anything really would, perhaps even could, be changed. What man could convince the sun to stay up past two p.m. in winter? They were born in this place, on these high plains, and it put short borders around the territory of hope. Yet, Tom believes in something better. A little better, anyway.

In spring, the mayor likes to drive around spotting bellies. It is frustrating to be a single man in a moment such as this. Tom cannot participate in his own game. But still, he feels personally responsible for each of those fetuses, as if he is their godfather. If not for him, the world would have less life in it, less actual life. He is always a little surprised when the women do not come up to him and offer their thanks.

But the mayor had not thought of how long the middle would feel. He had only considered the beginning and the end. Like two cans with a string tied between them, conception and birth connected in a way that is both miraculous and plain. For the mayor, who has no everyday miracle taking place in his own house, who eats leftover pizza for breakfast and runs on the treadmill in his basement and wades through the city council meeting and has lunch with the football coach, the wait is frustrating and overlong. He worries that by the time he gets to the end, the story will not be his anymore, that when he proudly stands up and announces the dozens of lives born of his imagination, everyone will be at home, coddling babies they consider, wrongly, Tom thinks, their own.

FOR MARTHA, too, the middle is a very long space of time. In it, she tracks the disappointments. At first, she does this in order to make counterarguments, to explain to her baby that yes, it is dark almost all day long in winter, but in summer, you don't have to sleep at all, I will never force you to go to bed. Instead, we will all three climb up on the roof and lie on our backs in bathing suits, tanning at nine at night.

IN THE WINDOWS: women change shape and men change shape, too, and then feel angry with themselves for it. It's the fat of sympathy building up, the men think. Devotion.

Really, it is boredom and bad weather and probably would have happened anyway. Across the street from Martha and Jeff's, Fat Henderson again stands in profile, naked, observing his inglorious facade.

Tom sits out on the two-hearted bench alone, sliding into the middle with no one to drift closer to. In the square appears a nurse he hired to talk to what he imagined would be a throng of expectant parents. She is carrying a paperback novel under her arm and breathing on her hands to warm them.

The mayor goes over. "Hello, Ms. Walker," he says. "Thank you for coming." He motions to a podium he has dragged out from his office along with a series of connected extension cords and a microphone.

"I have the right day?" she asks. "I thought you said you had advertised."

"I'm sorry. Would you like to give the talk anyway?"

"No one is here."

THE NURSE WALKS UP to the microphone. On the small black amplifier beside her, she flips a switch and taps the microphone to test it. Her eyes flicker over to the mayor every few seconds, asking a very obvious question.

"So," the nurse says. She waits for someone to relieve her. "It's not very good to drink when you are pregnant." The mayor smiles warmly, nods.

"Husbands who smoke should do so outside." The nurse's voice booms out like some god of boring advice. And truly, no one passes. Not girls with rounded bellies, not young men, not old women, not children. It is as if the streets have been cleared in preparation for a terrible storm, a bomb threat, an asteroid headed straight this way. No matter how tightly tucked the nurse's brow, Tom just smiles at her. *Tell the world what you know,* his eyes say.

"It's getting dark now," the nurse says. "I think I'll pack up and go home." It starts to snow. The low sun makes everything seem suddenly brighter for a moment before it shuts the light out altogether. The mayor feels that they are in a very old place, dust gathering around them, hundreds of years passing while the nurse folds her notes back into her book and brushes the flakes off her fake-fur collar.

"Thank you," he says. "It was helpful." He means it. She realizes this, and it makes her just sad enough to hold his hand a little longer than she would have otherwise.

IN THE WEEK before June twelfth, four babies arrive in all their pudgy, yowling glory. The mayor makes a special point of showing up to meet them all, have their pictures taken, commemorate the moment despite its lack of prize-winningness.

On June eleventh, Martha feels the first contractions and goes to the hospital after several hours of pacing, rocking, getting in and out of the shower, the bath. In the maternity ward, the miracle of life is an everyday occurrence, a job to be completed and cleaned up from. One of the nurses brought in muffins. Someone is watching a talk show in another room, loud. The pain never lets up completely, just changes intensity. Sometimes Martha is not sure she can breathe. The nurses look at her, bored by her anguish.

At 11:00 p.m. on the night before the winning day, the wrestling coach and Nathalie arrive, he pulling her by the elbow. She has felt no contractions, not even a twinge, but he thinks maybe a change of scenery will help get things started.

"See, baby?" he says to her belly. "You are in the hospital now. Time to come out. You only have twenty-four hours."

The nurses refuse to give them a room so Nathalie sits in a plastic chair and drinks soda while the wrestling coach hovers outside Martha's room with his watch in his hand, observing the minutes tick. "Come on, come on, come on," he says to the minute hand, coaxing it to slow down. If he has a chance of winning the car he needs this other baby to be born in the next fifty-two minutes, on June eleventh. The mayor joins him, his own watch in his hand. "Come on, come on, come on," he prays to his watch, begging it to speed up. God, should he be following this small drama, is going to have to choose a side. He waits as 11:15 turns to 11:35. Martha is pushing. She is crying. At 11:47, the baby crowns. And at 11:58 p.m., he is born. The baby, two minutes shy of a prizewinner, cries. Martha does not even check the clock, cannot consider the time. Her husband allows himself one small glance, but his heart only sinks so far before the tossing fists of his son buoy it. The wrestling coach does a robot dance down the hall to celebrate.

NATHALIE DOES NOT go into labor. No one goes into labor. For the first time in the hospital staff's memory, the ward is silent. The mayor walks the halls, saying, "You never know. Any minute." The wrestling coach knocks on his wife's belly like it is a door behind which someone has overslept his alarm. The nurses drink coffee and read gossip magazines. The muffins dwindle. "You should have more contests," they say. "In a town as unlucky as this one, it will guarantee us the day off." And indeed, it does. On June twelfth, no babies are born. There isn't even another close call, a team to cheer for. Tom wonders how they're doing in Russia. He imagines a shiny new Lada Niva sitting outside the hospital awaiting its new owners.

Seeing that her husband will not allow her to go home, the nurses finally let Nathalie into a room, only so she can fall asleep.

MARTHA LOOKS AT her baby, who knows nothing yet of the world waiting: corruption, bribery, teenage drivers, being flat-footed, having too little money and too much beer, doing the dishes, going out for dinner and being disappointed in the overboiled spaghetti sauce, getting up for work before light, coming home after sunset, the roses wilting on the table, the list of jobs that need doing around the house: cleaning the tiny screen on the faucet, breaking down the boxes your aunt sent and writing a thank-you note for the terrible-smelling bubble bath that was inside, scrubbing the frozen-on pink sticky in the refrigerator. This is life. Barring environmental or political catastrophe, Martha expects the world her child lives in to look much like this one. It can be difficult to see the miracle in it. To her bundle, she offers an out clause: you were born, innocent and beautiful and straight from the lips of God, but if you look around and see the potholed streets, the mud puddles, the old nurses in too much makeup, and you decide you want to be an angel instead, I will understand. I will wrap you in a soft blanket, cover you up completely and allow you to make your decision in private. If I open the blanket and you are gone, evaporated, I will forgive you for it. But if you are still there, pink and fussing, I will know that you have chosen to stay, to endure the old world. And I will try to teach you the tricks to make it easier. How to get on the bus without buying a ticket; how to pay for one movie and see three; how to fight with your father so that you always win; how to ensure maximum darkening of the skin in the sun; how to find your life's horizon—that place just far enough in the distance to keep you moving forward but not so far as to be discouraging. "For my part," Martha says aloud, "I will give you food when you are hungry and warmth when you are cold. Let's start with that promise. I'll swear to it, my love, I will cross my tired heart." She folds the blanket loosely over her infant until she can't see him anymore.

OUTSIDE, the Ford's red bow is slumped and bleached. The car is a minor celebration in front of an old blocky hospital. None of this went as planned, yet somehow Tom feels fulfilled. He was part of something, if only on the periphery. In the morning, he will give the car to Martha for being the closest, and Martha will sell it to the wrestling coach for a good price and put the money away. It will be enough to buy plane tickets to someplace warm every winter until the baby is grown. She does not need a car—for transportation, Martha has feet and the bus.

Light, heat, now those are worth paying for.

The Cape
of Persistent
Hope

Mother Land

The African fell asleep just after dusk and woke at dawn. In late summer, when Lucy had met him in Los Angeles, this was reasonable. Long days, short nights. By mid-October, she felt half abandoned. She lay down with him at five in the afternoon, tried breathing exercises, sheep-counting exercises, but what she did instead was worry. Her dead mother rose up over her like a full moon, and Lucy saw ungood developments: dead skin crumbling like old paper, her breasts were dripping from her. Lucy thought of her unmoored balloon of a mother, naked and fat, hovering over the entire earth. Little children would scream and point. Men would turn away. Beauty queens would pray, "Not me, not me."

Lucy's mother had moved back to her childhood home of Beirut when she retired but instead of a long life there, her mother had died. Lucy did not see her die. Her sister had gone, and her sister was too good a daughter to compete with. The sister had called Lucy and tried to explain what was happening, but Lucy wanted off the phone. She muted everything that wasn't her own bright young life.

All summer Lucy had not slept, and the African had, and he woke at dawn and made coffee and ate half a loaf of bread, toasted to a dry crack. By the time she got up, his day was already half over. He was yawning by lunch.

She said, "By solstice, we'll hardly see each other."

"It's natural to rise with the sun."

"Natural if you're an elephant, if you're a caveman." Lucy flicked the lights on and off.

He did not concede.

"This is something to leave you over," she told him. "This is a good reason."

The African opened the refrigerator and took out a jar of Marmite. He scooped his finger and sucked the tar-slick off. He looked at Lucy up and down, as if he was trying to decide how much trouble she was worth. When she was twelve, she had walked from her house to the market with a short list from her mother and it had been peaceful. When she was thirteen, every pickup blew its horn. The drivers whistled. One year, you're a kid with a carton of milk; the next, you are a body, visible to everyone.

"I have a better idea than you leaving me. I should look in on my house in Africa anyway. Let's move to the equator. Let's get day and night even again."

THE DIFFERENCE BETWEEN staying home and going far away was keeping her blood in the familiar river or diverting it. Lucy had never before thought about her own city or her own bloodline and the people she could marry who would leave it unchanged. When she told him about her boyfriend, her father said, "An African?" and Lucy comforted him, "He's white, Dad."

"A white African?" She felt for the first time the curvature of the earth below her, the idea that she could slip across it like a bead of water, join a different, greener pool.

Lucy thought about the African's proposition at a café where a group of Scandinavian boys made their foreignness obvious with shorts that were too long or pants that were too short. *And don't they sell any other kinds of shoes in Europe?* Lucy thought. But she liked the idea of being the foreigner. She liked the idea that she could succumb, that she could be entirely surrounded, an island washed by unfamiliar waves. She remembered a story she had read as a girl of a white woman on the dark continent, a great adventurer, befriending lions and elephants and members of the various benign tribes. She imagined becoming a new person. She liked the idea of doing something that would make her perfect sister nervous. She would take up making art. A woman artist in a strange land. Dangerous and friendly creatures, dangerous and friendly people, coffee plantations and furious rivers and the story of man. She could get into drinking gin. She could, as a PBS television show had once instructed her, learn about apes and discover what it meant to be human.

She wanted advice and her fingers had dialed her mother's number before she remembered: dead. "Hello?" said a woman on the other end.

"Mom?"

"Hi, sweetheart."

"Mom?"

"Yes, it's me. It's me, honey. Darlene?"

Lucy almost hung up. She almost said, "Wrong number, sorry." But the feeling of having a mother on the other end of the line hit her bloodstream like alcohol. "How are you?" she asked, and it was a gift when the woman began to talk about the gardeners and the bald patch they'd left in the yard and then the vomiting cat and then the good deal on those French green beans Dad likes and the dream she had about trying to sweep the kitchen floor with a toothbrush. Lucy held her breath so she didn't give herself away. She did not say *Mmm* or *Uh-huh* or *Yes* or *That's funny.*

"What did you end up deciding about your trip?" the woman asked.

"My trip?" Lucy said, and then without waiting for a reply: "I'm going. I love you."

Lucy let her head fall into her hands and felt their mugginess, their dirty salt. *I'm going,* she repeated to herself.

The African bought the tickets that night. Two seats to the other side of everything.

In bed: "You're not really African, though," Lucy had said, looking at his big white arms.

"That's where I'm from. What else would I be?"

"But you're really European."

"And before that, we're all African. Even you, sweet woman." That was the way with the African—it was one big, plentiful world.

THEY WERE MET at the airport by a driver who told them on the ride home all about the floods last summer and the way the land had changed because of them. "Now it's so dry," he said. Lucy looked out the window. Women in patterned cloth skirts, men in jeans. Everywhere, brightly colored plastic tubs in stacks. Children played in a red dirt field wearing their navy-and-white uniforms. *Are they poor?* she wanted to ask the African. Where should she set her sorry-gauge? The people looked clean and tended to. They looked fed. Lucy wanted to see wild animals by the side of the road, but all she saw were dogs, dozens, ribs and the spaces between, long of tongue.

The house was huge. "My father was a diplomat," the African said. He introduced her to the staff who all had uniforms and called her "ma'am."

"Have these people been here all the time you were in LA?"

"Of course. They've been with the family for years. It's normal here to have help and not expensive. Plus you can't leave an empty house for security reasons." They sat on the veranda and ate beef stew with a thick pasty mash of vegetables and the local root, and they drank cold beer. "Welcome to Africa," the African said. He leaned down and pressed his lips to her forehead, but what Lucy felt was his beard, which had grown in over the long day of travel. The sunset was momentary—a sweet flash and then dark. "Time for bed," the African said. Lucy's body was unclocked and restless. Her eyes were dry but she wanted more to drink. "Stay with me for a while," she said, but he had come for the sleep and he wanted to sleep it. He had come for the twelve hours of light, twelve hours of dark. He looked at Lucy like she was asking him to remove a semi-essential body part, lend it to her for no good reason.

"It's dark," he said. "We're already missing it."

GARDENERS TENDED THE GARDEN. Drivers drove. Maids did the wash, changed the sheets every day, mopped the floors. The house was open, what Lucy was sure the African's mother would have described to her English friends as "gracious." The big windows looked out at the lawn with its short knots of grass and the jungle leaning in. There were red flowers like big mouths. Lucy tried to pour orange juice and a woman said, "What is it you'd like, ma'am?" She took off her clothes to shower, and they were gone when she got out and new ones laid out on the bed. The first set would be washed, pressed, folded by the end of the day.

Lucy wanted to call someone, but her sister thought she was stupid and that this plan was stupid and Lucy did not want to hear why. Her father was angry that she had left. There wasn't anyone who wanted to know what it smelled like where she was, what she'd eaten or dreamed.

The daytime was big and empty. The African wanted to help his neighbor rebuild a wall that had been flooded out. Lucy set up a ball of clay in an upstairs bedroom with a view over the trees to the weepingly green hills. There had been elephants living there not long ago. She could easily picture them, searching the earth with their trunks, spiraling good grasses up to their mouths. Lucy put on a white shirt and untied the clay bag. "OK," she said. "Sculpt." She wanted to be a person capable of making things, of creating beauty. She made a sticky sphere, hollowed it. She thumb-pressed the bowl, tried to make it big enough to hold something. A stream of ants crossed the windowsill, fat as a rope, liquid almost, searching.

————

THE AFRICAN RELISHED the even split of the day and night. He felt exactly as rested as he was productive. Lucy hid a sketchbook beneath her pillow, brought it out once the African was asleep. She drew fat-leafed trees and grasses. She drew sky and ground. It looked lush and warm, the kind of place where the air was thick and jasmine-scented, where you were grateful for each sip in your lungs. She wanted to put a person in the scene, someone to appreciate the beauty, but each time she tried, the figure looked flat. Lucy erased and retried, and the paper grew thin.

LUCY WALKED UPSTAIRS in the big house and then downstairs. She sat outside and ate a mango. She wondered what her sister was doing now that she was out of their mother's orbit. They hadn't spoken since the end. She went inside and stood in the kitchen for a long time. She wasn't hungry, but she wanted something. When the African came in sweat-skunky, put his work-proud hands on her butt, she turned and said, "I'm bored."

The idea was his. The ultimate sculpture project: build-

ing something inside, doubling, doubling until a baby un-
curls like a fern. It seemed that all he had to do was speak
the idea and she was pregnant already. It scared Lucy, how
easily it had happened. As if they had been walking all this
time under a canopy dripping in embryos. Now that she
knew, she was afraid to look up, to raise her hand above her
head and accidentally knock another free.

Lucy did not tell her father that she was pregnant. He
expected marriage first and she could not imagine marrying this man—not here, not in this distant place. She did
not want to buy a white dress in a dusty market. She did not
want an American wedding in an African church or an
African wedding in which she was the pale, false bride.
There was no ceremony in which she made sense so she
kept the news a secret.

The months passed and the inner sculpture did not
make Lucy's clay any more generous. She had thought of
art as a house you simply had to unlock: she had been one
of the good artists in school, always an A student, and she'd
thought that the creations would pour forth if she only had
the time and space, and here she was in this new universe
with all the hours of the day, but now there was a new
problem: none of this belonged to her and she did not trust
her own eyes here. She made various bowls, none of them

necessary for the world. She hadn't thought about the need for a kiln and everything she'd put on the porch to dry the day before dissolved in this morning's dew. The African came into the room and said, "How is the little foreigner?"

"Tired," she said. "Untalented."

"I was talking about someone else." He staked a claim on her belly with his hands. "But I'm glad to hear how you feel."

"I feel moved-into."

"Let's go on holiday. I'll take you to the animals."

THEY WAITED FOR the tiny airplane on the ground under a mango tree mad with fruit. Behind them, a man waited for customers in his small open-air café. Six plastic tables, a television tuned to a preacher, a Coke machine sweating. When the African went to the bathroom the man smiled at Lucy and she thought he was flirting until he looked at her rounding belly and asked about the baby. She had almost forgotten—more than by any legal marriage, any symbolic ring, a pregnant woman was marked as another man's property.

Lucy picked the brightest fruit, bit the end and rolled the skin back. Her face was yellow and sticky. The African watched her with pleasure. This was exactly the kind of woman he preferred to love—fertile, juice-sweet. He came in and kissed her, the mess of her lips. They heard the plane, watched it grow bigger in the clear blue. It skidded and, so small and light, bounced to a stop.

"We just walk right up?" Lucy asked. And they did, wearing their sunglasses, stepping over the weeds in the tarmac, ready to take flight. On board, the pretty young flight attendant poured beer.

"Thanks, sweetheart," the African said. Lucy was surprised that she liked this, the old-fashioned racism and sexism of a big white man sweet-talking a small dark woman. It felt good to admit that power was unequal, that, if he wanted to, the African could pick them both up and carry them away. Then her hand went to her middle. *Don't be a girl,* she thought. *But don't be a boy, either.*

IT RAINED ALL NIGHT, the kind of warm rain that made Lucy feel the distance she had come. Even in summer in California, the rain was cold. She listened to it on the thatch of their little cabin, the crack around the door frame weeping. The African lit all three kerosene lamps and dealt the cards, but he couldn't keep track of any of her rules and she couldn't keep track of his. He put a jacket over his head—he never wore a raincoat, only used it to make a roof—and ran to the restaurant where he bought stewed chicken with soft flatbreads for dipping. The food was hot and rich and Lucy ate her portion and sent him for another. All the while, rain.

The African said. "Pregnancy is good for you. You look more natural now."

"Natural?"

"You know the most famous Lucy in Africa is an ancient skeleton? They've found older bones now, but your namesake is important proof of evolution. The shape of her spine meant she walked upright."

"You want me to look more like a Neanderthal?"

"Wrong continent, wrong age, darling. Lucy was a hominid."

The African was hungry for her all night. In half sleep and half love, she heard something outside tearing up the grass and chewing it. *Cows,* she thought. Except for the rain and the thatch hut, she could almost place herself in the Midwest, a farmhouse and a grain silo nearby, a herd of Jerseys heavy with milk.

———

IN THE MORNING, the net was black with mosquitoes. Lucy flicked her finger and watched them take off, their fat legs dangling below. "How are we ever going to get out of bed?"

The African made a case for staying, but Lucy said, "Take me to see a giraffe. I've been in Africa seven months."

The footprints outside their door were huge disks. "Hippos," the African said. "They come out of the lake at night to graze." Ordinary, his voice said. As if he were talking about skunks, raccoons. She thought of them in their little hut, naked while a herd of giants tore at the ground just outside. Lucy and the African walked from their cabin under the massive trees. The hotel owner served them oily pancake-bread and jam and sweet Indian tea in an open-air room, wood-floored and thatched. The room was cool and dark, the walls washed with blue. There were chickens somewhere nearby, clucking. Lucy swatted at her ankles, hot with bites. All that extra blood in her body, sucked out.

Another couple came and sat at the next table. "Having a blessed morning?" the man said. He was wearing all khaki the way white people did here. They were missionaries, the man said, without invitation and without embarrassment. Lucy thought people had given this up, mostly, the conversion of darker people to a lighter God. Or at least that they disguised it underneath the pretense of medicine or education. The man went on to talk about what he called "The Jesus Movie" as if this was something every good soul on earth knew well. Lucy pictured a tired VHS tape, thirty years old, its ribbon stretched and the audio slowed down. A man on a cross plus your sins and the sins of your continent equals no more struggle. The woman smiled hard but said nothing. She looked to Lucy like she would rather be shopping for sensible separates in Cleveland. Like she would rather be living the Christian life in a house with central air and a shorn lawn.

Lucy said to her, "Sometimes I just wish I could eat ham and eggs for breakfast."

"Mary can't speak," the man said. "She's a mute."

"I'm so sorry."

"Nothing to apologize for. God works in mysterious ways," he said. "She is our family's pillar. I don't need her to speak to know I can lean on her."

Two snarl-faced monkeys hung from the tree branches above, impatient for scraps. They had long black arm hair and gray-leathered feet. Lucy noticed a baby on one of their backs, clinging. Little eyes, little mouth, long fingers. Lucy tore her bread in half and pretended to drop it on the ground. "Oops," she said to the mama monkey, who let go of her branch, her mouth opening wild and red, and fell the fifteen feet, her hair rising, her baby clinging. Lucy waited for the fall, the crack of bones. The monkey landed on her feet, soundless. She grabbed the bread and swung from railing to branch to branch in no seconds. Lucy watched as the monkey ate the bread, tear by tear. She did not feed even one piece to her baby.

The missionary told the African about his plan to buy a bush plane so he could reach the most needy tribes, so remote that they might otherwise go completely unsaved. His voice cracked with excitement and Lucy could practically see the picture behind his eyes: him in the rumble of his own propellers, his mute wife at his side, hovering like a tiny God over a patch of savage earth.

No one asked if Lucy and the African needed salvation that morning. Maybe their skin color meant it was assumed that they already had the right god in their hearts, or maybe their skin color made it impolite to ask.

Above, the monkeys shook the branches, hungry for more.

————

TOURISTS WOULD HAVE SEEN the animals in their own private safari vans, but the couple took a local bus to the game park because that's what Africans did. It was a minibus, ten seats, and Lucy and the African took two seats in the middle. She swung her bag around to the front so she could hold it, and left it strapped around her back. She thought she was managing not to look nervous. The driver, a giant man, stayed outside, hustling for fares even after all ten seats were full. In the dirt parking lot, women carried trays of fruit on their heads, sliced and in plastic bags. Others had watches, others orange-colored breads, others chewing gum. Men on the bus—Lucy was the only woman, she noticed—slipped their windows open and threw money onto the trays, snapped the tabs on soda cans and drank the contents in one sip.

"Where we're going is a private reserve," the African said. "No predators, so we can walk around instead of being in one of those horrid safari trucks. Just have to watch for hippos."

Lucy snorted when she laughed and some of the men in the truck turned to look at her.

"I'm serious," he said. "The hippopotamus is the most dangerous animal in the jungle. They are easily startled and their jaws are very strong." He snapped his hand shut. Lucy could not tell if he was torturing or teasing her.

"What if I had gone outside last night when they were grazing?" she asked. "Why didn't you tell me before?"

"But you didn't."

It got hot on the bus. Lucy felt as if she was breathing other people's air, direct from their muggy lungs. She put her face to the crack in the window. A woman got on, finally another woman, and she had a canvas sack that was wriggling. Lucy thought: *snakes*. Then: *children*. She scolded herself. Do not mistrust these people. They are black, and black is beautiful. This phrase, a stowaway from the cover of a glossy magazine in the airport someplace, kept echoing in her brain. She was constantly afraid that she would say it aloud by accident. It felt like a small landmine in the rocky earth of her head.

The African, all this time, was reading a newspaper, as comfortable as if he were sitting in the lobby of a big hotel in Nairobi, someplace designed to make white people feel good about this continent, where the desk was staffed with polite, good-looking blacks, the bar made of wood from endangered trees, ringed with the sweat of highball glasses.

The canvas sack crowed and Lucy almost laughed with relief. "Buy me a drink?" she said to the African. He found a bill in his pocket and handed it to her without taking his eyes off the paper. *No*, she wanted to say, *you do it*. The soda woman was not far away, but Lucy did not want to call to her. She put her long white arm out into the bright sky and all the eyes went to it, took a step away like it was a deformity. Then a man with a plastic bucket took the bill and replaced it with a small plastic bag. "Peanuts for the lady," he said. Lucy looked at the bag. "Thank you," she told him.

"I thought you were thirsty," the African said.

THE BUS DRIVER GOT ON, finally, and began to drive. He steered and shifted with one hand, while, with the other, he held a bouquet of barbecued chicken skewers from which he took large bites. In a minute, they stopped and picked up three more women who sat on the laps of men in the back. A minute after that, there were two men, two small boys and a woman with a baby standing by the road. Lucy waited for the driver to explain that another bus was on its way, but instead, his helper opened the door and let them all in. The woman with the baby pressed her butt into the African's face and Lucy tried to make herself small. Air was less and less available.

Then the bus came to a short stop in the middle of the road and everybody started to talk at once. Young men and old, thick as a swarm, fell against the bus with their fists, yelled into the windshield and windows. The men and boys surrounded them completely. The African looked up from his paper. "Fuck," he said. Lucy held her bag tighter. A man with a moon-flat face spit on her window. Her heart felt like a bicycle wheel, turning over and over. She wanted to be small, but she was big. She was big and bright. She felt like a star. Someone had seen her get on, phoned his cousins, she thought. White people, rich people, traveling slowly over land, their pockets fat with the cash necessary to see exotic vegetarian animals. The African said something in Swahili to the woman with the baby. Lucy leaned into him. "What?" she asked. The men and boys outside began to shake the bus back and forth. It rocked so easily. It rocked like it had been designed to do just that. The people on the bus yelled back to those outside the bus. The driver threw the last of his chicken skewers out the window. Everything was noise.

Any town, anywhere on earth had a ditch to dump a girl's body into. Lucy's mother's ghost was either omniscient and would not need to be told about her daughter's murder, or she was nothing more than rotted bones. Lucy thought of the call to her father made by some local policeman. So this was how he would find out about his grandchild. She imagined him and her sister, the two left, alone together. Maybe, she thought, trying to create a little pool of hope, I am worth more alive than dead. Ransom. The baby might be valuable. She was grateful for the baby; it was the first time she had felt that way.

When Lucy was a child she had been taken to a therapist after admitting to her mother that she dreamed constantly of drowning. The therapist had instructed her to imagine a safe place, say a quiet meadow in the mountains, wildflowers and small rabbits and a warm, cloudless sky. She had understood the idea, but the meadow never worked on her. There were bears there, there were wolves, the ground was full of stinging bugs and briars and she was very far from home.

As the bus shook and the men yelled, Lucy knew she was going to die. She closed her eyes and she wished she could go home. What she pictured, what home turned out to be, was the westbound 10 freeway slithering above Los Angeles. There was traffic in her fantasy, medium-heavy but the cars were still moving. It was three p.m. traffic, the worst still to come. This was the reason everyone who had ever left LA gave for their departure—the gray rivers, no one ever where they wanted to be. Lucy could hear her tires bump over the freeway's ridges, she could hear the public radio news theme song, she could see the white license plates with two palm trees. She could see the pale sky and knew the shock of the ocean was ahead, sudden and blue at the edge of the city. Her blood slowed down, her breathing.

The African grabbed Lucy's hand and began to stand up. She wanted to tuck deeper into the corner, if anything. Not to expose more of her colorless, overbright body, not to move through the crowd. She resisted but he tugged and got her to stand. They pushed through the men and women, the sweat and breath of them, their arms and necks and elbows. The bus shook. The men and boys outside yelled and the open door was not a welcome light but a pathway into the fury. The African descended the steps and Lucy imagined the fists on their faces, in their stomachs. She imagined the baby being pummeled.

The men and boys who were thin and fat, wearing T-shirts and jeans, plastic sandals, continued to yell and they continued to throw their bodies at the bus and to pull at its windows, but they did not fall upon Lucy and the

African. They moved aside for the couple to pass through. Lucy was the only thing she had not considered: meaningless. There was so much air. Lucy sucked it back. The African smiled at her like they had not been about to die.

"I don't understand what's going on," she said.

"Oh, sorry, I forget you don't speak the language. It was a protest. A fisherman died in the lake and they want the government to dredge the body up. So they blocked the road, but the driver wanted the fares. It's no problem. We can walk the rest of the way."

A huge lake appeared for the first time in front of them. It was wide and silver. Lucy had imagined her body being thrown into the trench, but now she knew it would have been the lake. Of course it would have.

While she tried to slow her breathing, to re-believe that no one here had ever wanted to harm her, that they hardly even registered her existence, Lucy thought of a fisherman, carp-pecked and coming apart in the silt. It was too early to be feeling the baby kick. Probably it was indigestion, but Lucy put her hands on her belly and held them there. The traveler was quiet. What stranger world was there than inside this body, what more alien landscape? A foreigner inside a foreigner. The hills on one side of them were bright red and the acacia trees looked like they belonged in a diorama of Africa. There were stocky gray horses in the distance.

The African said, "Don't worry, I'll tell you when to be afraid."

If the baby was to be born here, as she would be, mother and child would not share a home. California would still exist and Lucy would take the child back and show her where her mother had grown up and they would keep watch for famous people and ride the Ferris wheel on the pier and dig their feet into the hot sand until they reached the cool, sea-wet layers beneath. But the girl would want to go home because the Pacific would not be her ocean. Because she would be hungry for her own earth and her own sky. Lucy, faraway Lucy, carried in her exact middle a creature who already belonged here, a whole watershed of veins that ran with this place.

"If we had gone someplace where both of us were strangers we would always have been far away together," she said. It could have been Ecuador, an island chain in Asia. She imagined walking down a dirt track just like this one, only there would be bamboo forests and rice paddies and whole families on a single bicycle and Lucy and the African would both misunderstand the culture together. They would be the same kind of outsider.

"I need to tell my sister about the baby. I need to tell my father," she said.

"Why haven't you?"

"I don't know. My parents were immigrants and my dad spent his life trying to be American. I felt guilty that he would have a foreign grandchild."

"All babies are foreigners," the African said. "None of us knows what we're going to get. Isn't that the beauty?"

They came to the park's gate and paid their money and the three of them, the family, set out into the wild together. There were huge red cliffs ahead of them and a green savanna. The horses were not horses, Lucy realized. Now she saw the stripes. "Zebras?" she said, disbelieving. The black-and-white of them was right there. No fence, no boundary. There was no separation between human and animal. All any of them were was skin and fur, muscle and oxygen, the ability to eat, to run, to raise their young.

"Lion food," the African said. "Their color is their only defense. A group of zebras," he told her, pleased to know the rules, "is called a dazzle."

Departure Lounge

We lived in a bubble on a crater on a mountain on an island in the middle of the Pacific Ocean, but where we imagined we lived was Mars. The top of Mauna Loa in Hawaii was the closest place on earth to that distant red planet so that was where we moved through a domed world with airlocks and decontamination zones and wore space suits whenever we went outside. I was just the chef, there to provide nourishment to the astronauts-in-training. A glorified cafeteria lady.

A few miles below were thousands of families who had hauled their winter-pale bodies across the sea and stripped down to bathing suits, their skin shy and prickly in the first waves. These vacationers ordered the umbrella drink, ate the papaya, flayed themselves out on the beach and joyfully let the sun burn them.

That was not my Hawaii. I cooked the meals and looked out at the horizon and imagined that I was a year's journey from my own planet, 249 million miles from everything I knew. That the only lives were those of my crewmates. That what we had to eat, our water, our habitat, was the only place left to us. That we would die here.

THE REST OF MY CREWMATES were astronauts-in-training. They had entered and won a contest to be the first people to live on Mars. They were young and could run forty miles and had science degrees and high IQs and good temperaments and in interview after interview they had each expressed their willingness to give up all the pleasures of Earth to die in outer space. Theirs was a one-way mission. If they made it to Mars at all, and they might well not, they would live the rest of their days on a planet inhospitable to human life. They would have to hope that the food that scientists believed would grow on Mars really did grow on Mars. They would have to hope that nothing went wrong with the water supply. They would be radiated by a too-close sun and there would be no hospital to treat their cancers.

Theirs would be names children would memorize in school. John, who had run in the Olympics; Marcy, who had been to MIT; Brit, the brilliant immigrant from a war-torn country in Central Africa; Sherman, whose grandfather had been a famous physicist; Jack, an artist who had shown at the Whitney; and Sunshine, who had lived in the Amazon rain forest canopy for a year studying frogs and who told me late one night after more wine than we were supposed to drink that she had tried to break off her engagement with the person she had loved since she was fourteen when she learned she had been chosen, but he had insisted they get married anyway, that he would be faithful even after she left for the outer reaches of their solar system. She told me that she was looking forward to being alone.

"What about you?" she had asked. "Tell me your story."

Mine was the most unremarkable story: I was a girl from a tiny town in Minnesota who'd followed the sun to California and now Hawaii. I had just been through an unremarkable divorce with no heroism involved—my ex and I were two earthlings who were no longer good together. "I'm just here to cook," I had said. "You are the mission; I am the sustenance."

Did the food make the day's work possible? Was it heavy in the heart or the gut? That was my job. This freeze-dried broccoli warmed in a pool of fake cheese and pasta. This glass of Tang, the only bright color left.

AS IT TURNED OUT, living in fake space was no less tiring than living on Earth. The astronauts were too cheerful, too serious, too invested. They critiqued every single thing I cooked, examined my attempt at an approximation of Kung Pao Chicken and found the texture depressing. "Yes," I said, "because freeze-dried meat is terrible and Kung Pao is not even a real Chinese dish, but I'm supposed to give you American comfort."

Six weeks into a five-month stay and I was already a bad Martian. If I were on the real mission, I would be the person who drove her rover into the red dust of a storm and never returned. I would be the first death in the colony.

One night I found Peter, whom I had briefly dated in college, on the internet. We typed our lives back and forth. *Happy, happy, happy,* we both wrote at first. *I'm doing great! I'm living in a simulated Martian landscape! My job is to make the least depressing dishes with the most depressing ingredients!*

He said: *I bought a house and this really soft rug from Iran! My sister is getting married and says hello! Wait, did I ever tell you that I'm gay?!*

I said: *Yes, love, I think we all knew that,* though I hadn't.

And then the notes began to include more: his mother's death, my divorce. Finally, he wrote: *I wish I had a child.* That was the whole letter. One of ten trillion truths. Not, I wish I lived in a nicer house. I wish my father was alive. I wish my neighbors upstairs would stop rocking in their rocking chairs. I wish for a vacation. *I wish I had a child.*

It sounded like a project. It sounded like a reason. It sounded like a better escape than the one in which I currently found myself. In the morning, I found another note: *I'm coming to Hawaii for a few days. I'll wave up at the mountain at you.*

I looked out the porthole-shaped window at Sunshine in her space suit, kneeling in the dust of a perfectly good planet, spooning samples into a vial. I thought of the dozens of pounds of dried cheese I was supposed to turn into sustenance and the weeks ahead of me in my tiny bunk with these other lives as they prepared to hurtle themselves into space and I prepared for the continuation of my plain life. Before noon, I had done the calculations and figured out I would be ovulating on about day four of Peter's visit.

IT WAS AS SIMPLE a task as I had ever completed—I served the bad dinner I had made and then I walked out through the airlocked doors, not wearing a space suit. I heard John yell out to me, "What the *fuck* are you doing?" and I called back, "Problem solve, Astronaut John!" I went past the failing plant nursery, past the lab dome and down the mountain. It was night and cold and I hadn't been outside without a space suit in six weeks. The air, the Earth air, was unspeakably good. It got warmer as I descended and the foliage changed until it was green and lush, and everything smelled like flowers and I stopped to pick a mango off a tree and peeled it with my teeth and ate it, the juice covering my hands and face. *This planet,* I thought. *Holy shit, this planet.*

PETER SAID, "I know we're in Hawaii and I should take you to some luau, but I'm really craving German food. Do you mind?"

"I will eat anything that doesn't come out of a package. Anything." We ate schnitzel and dumplings, good pickles. I looked at Peter through the amber and bubble-columned beer. He was handsome through it, warm. The distortion did a good thing to his face. I felt amped up, like I had escaped prison and someone was going to come and drag me back and I had to enjoy every second of freedom.

Peter said, "Do you remember in college when you and that redhead stole a groundskeeper's golf cart and ran it into the ditch?" These were the exact stories I wished to forget. Hilarious in the dining-hall morning, funny in the afternoon, but by evening all that was left were two girls with bruises on their shins, the silty residue of a hangover and a lot of homework left undone.

I said, "I forgot how pretty your eyes are."

"Thanks, kiddo," he told me.

There was fresh whipped cream on the apple strudel and I ate the whole dollop without offering to share. I thought of those poor jerks on the mountain who were will-fully walking away from everything beautiful around them. There were so many miraculous far-aways on this planet and yet they couldn't find enough to keep them here.

Peter said, "Weren't you happily married?"

I told him that the marriage had felt like carpentry, like sawdust and measuring and labor. My husband and I had tried at marriage every day—we had tried to keep open channels of communication and to show gratitude and give each other space to grow, all the things the inter-net told us to do. Every time the idea of babies had come up he had said, "Later? I don't feel like a father yet." I told Peter how, after eight years, I had come home after work covered in kitchen grime and gotten into the shower. It was late. The water was too hot and I wanted it that way. My husband had walked into the room in his boxers and said, "The problem isn't that I don't feel like a father, but that I don't want you to be the mother." I had looked at him through the glass door and the steam and he looked like a kid. "I wanted to think it was a matter of time," he had said. I had understood what he meant. There was no blowout. I had been too sad to be angry. He had taken his shorts off and gotten into the shower with me and we had stood there and looked at each other. We had known each other for our whole adult lives. We washed each other's backs and got out and in the morning we began to search for two new lives.

I looked at Peter and said, "I think I am ovulating and I think we should try to have a baby."

"Oh," he said. I knew I wasn't his ideal mate and maybe I wasn't his ideal womb either.

But Peter invited me up to his hotel room, as much question in his voice as answer. I inspected the toiletries bag in the bathroom, found it well stocked: expensive shaving cream, Band-Aids, Neosporin, arnica, a small bottle of white homeopathic pellets that said they treated hay fever. I ate three, letting them dissolve under my tongue. Back in the room the view was huge, the blue ocean and a streak of white beach and nothing else. I still felt like a space-person, exploring this expansive planet, a place with big marble bathrooms and deep soaking tubs and so much water.

Peter took out his phone, showed me a photo of him standing on top of a very tall mountain wearing those terrible zipper pants and those terrible wraparound sunglasses. He said, "I'm in good shape, see? I'm financially solvent. I'll be a really good dad. Are you serious that you'd do this for me?"

"It's not a gift," I said. "We'll share it. The baby, I mean."

He looked unsure. "Not like *together*. You don't have to pretend to like this," I said, gesturing to my body. "We are a results-oriented operation." Then he neck-kissed me. This kiss was soft. The word that came to my mind was "credible."

Sometimes I experience sex as something with its own geography, like a hike. This part is piney and the ground is brittle, now we come to a wildflower valley. This time it was just an act. We did only the necessary part and he kept his eyes closed and it didn't last long. After, lying side by side with a bowl of cold grapes, I imagined my body filled with those little swimmers, fast and strong, and the shimmering planet of the egg.

I thought about my ex-husband. There were noises associated with him: arguments and laughter, the moving of furniture. There was silence associated with him, too: breakfast without conversation, the two of us on the couch, the television on Mute. The silence I found myself in now was entirely different.

IN THE MORNING I sent an email to Sunshine to apologize. I had probably screwed up the whole operation.

Someone had to cook, make notes about recipes that worked and those that didn't. I imagined her sitting on her bunk on Mauna Loa, the photo of her and her sister standing on the beach with the Pacific behind them. I imagined her walking between airlocks to dinner where a plate of Kung Pao Chicken awaited her, fake upon fake, a fiction inside a fiction. I imagined that it made her happy instead of sad. I imagined that for her, it was all worth it.

Sunshine wrote, *It's a real fucking bummer that you took off. I'm giving up everything for this. I'm leaving true love behind. I'll never have kids. I'll never be a grandmother. It's called sacrifice for something bigger, something you obviously don't understand.*

I FLEW BACK across the ocean, moved into a new apartment in San Francisco and got work for a caterer cooking decent food with decent ingredients, and Peter went back to his life in LA. When I called to tell him about the series of negative pregnancy tests he said, "It takes time. I'm willing to keep trying if you are." We began our conjugal visits all over California. Each one was two days long and consisted of food and sex only. In Los Angeles we drove east and then came back to his apartment and took our clothes off, the taste of cricket tacos still on our tongues. We got dressed as soon as we were finished and sat in his living room and drank mint tea and I said, "What makes you want a baby anyway?" and he said, "Can you imagine how it must feel to love someone from the moment they begin to exist? To know that you'll never not love them?"

In September we ate skewers of solidified pork blood and bread crumbs. No baby. In October, we ate veal brains and got a room at a fancy hotel in San Francisco. No baby. In November, we went for sushi at a secret place with no sign. The urchin was hot-orange and slippery. The sushi chef brought another thing, a special thing and we each ate a piece of the pale, fatty fish. It tasted like seawater and butter.

"That is amazing," Peter said.

"Whale." The chef smiled, and put his finger to his lips. I got up and walked to the bathroom, imagining an animal a thousand times my size diving silently into the depths. I stood over the sink, wanting to throw up, but I couldn't make myself do it.

That night we did not try to make any babies. Peter slept with his arm over me, and even when my hip got sore and I wanted to turn over, I did not.

———

EACH MONTH, one blue line instead of two on the test. Each month I imagined a pinhead of life in my body, the beginnings of a person who could not simply break up with me and dash off to find a replacement. I would be a good mother. I would be generous and interested in all the side roads of childhood—superheroes and princesses and dinosaurs and bugs and minor weaponry and animal rights. I would mean it, if only someone would join me in my little life.

In June, I had an infestation of meal moths in my cupboards. They flew out whenever I opened the doors and I had to throw away all my food. There were little wormy babies in the hot-cereal box. Everything was hatching, except my own body.

In July, Sunshine and the rest of the crew emerged from fake Mars. There were television clips and tabloid stories with pictures of them walking out of the dome in their space suits, holding hands. As if they had completed something real. Sunshine was squinting. This was just the beginning. The first heroic mission in a series of heroic missions. Other scientists were building the ships and the housing and the greenhouses and the water purification systems, but these were the people who hoped to live and die on the red planet. These were our Martians and the television loved them. I wrote Sunshine an email welcoming her home and she wrote back, *This is not home. I won't be home until I get to Mars.*

I went walking that afternoon. Down the street, a teenage couple was sitting cross-legged on the sidewalk, leaning against someone's garage door, her in striped tights and him in all black. They were playing cards and laughing. I remembered being sixteen and feeling so in love with my friends that it seemed like they would be enough to sustain me for the rest of time. We wanted to be together all the time, six or eight of us, lying on someone's floor, pointing out shapes in the puckered ceiling as if the expanse above us were as beautiful as the heavens. We used to take showers together, showing off our new grown-up bodies like we were comparing gifts. We were young and slippery, more beautiful than we had the capacity to appreciate. We soaped each other up, and maybe we even kissed, girl and girl, boy and girl, but the kisses were just brass tokens, not redeemable for real prizes yet. On my street, I knelt down in front of the teenagers and said, "Stay as long as you can."

"We're not trespassing," the boy said. "This is public property."

I walked away fast, turned at the first chance I got. The street was lined with jacarandas, bare branches haloed in the purple fog of flowers.

IT SEEMED LIKE I might never get pregnant and I knew that I would lose Peter, too, if our project came to an end. I revived my online dating profile. I chatted with a guy named Todd. Poor Todd. He never did anything wrong, was probably a good man with bad taste in clothes. We went for pasta and I hated him before he opened his mouth.

I said, "Let's say you were going to run away, where would you go?"

He thought, hard. "Cancún."

"Seriously?" At least he hadn't said Mars.

He looked down at his lap, reddened, said, "Isn't it supposed to be nice there?" I started naming places: Kyrgyzstan, the Maldives, Siberia, Mozambique, and I could see that Todd's atlas was not coming into focus. "Wouldn't you want to go somewhere really, really far away?"

"Maybe for a week. But I like my life here. I have a nice house. I have a gym membership."

I didn't know where I would like my life. "Half of me wants to follow a handsome sheepherder across a mountain range, and half of me never wants to leave my apartment. You would be happy with a good tan and a bad tattoo."

"I hate tattoos," he said. "So you're wrong about all of it. You are a very sad person."

IN AUGUST, A newspaper clipping arrived in the mail with a note from Peter. *What if?* he wrote. The story was about a clinic in India where they take your eggs and sperm, mix them and then implant them into the uterus of an Indian woman who carries the child until term when you get on a flight and go pick up your baby. The women live together in a big house, all pregnant with blond, blue-eyed babies while their own husbands and children wait in their villages for the women to give birth and come home a little heavier and a little richer. I had two thoughts, which arrived at the exact same instant: *This is not OK* and *We will do this*. I called Peter immediately. "Let's," I said. "I want to."

"I didn't think you'd be into it," he said.

"I'm into it. I am going extinct." This made him laugh.

"It's nice to hear your voice," he told me, and I had to sit down.

———

THERE WERE PHONE CALLS across the seas. The doctor spoke perfect English with a soft British accent. She was soothing to talk to, someone who saw good outcomes from bad situations all the time. I was sure that her office was filled with the photos of new babies, the proof that science had outfoxed the imperfect human body. The first job was to choose a surrogate. The clinic emailed three photographs of smiling young women, one wearing a red sari, one wearing a green Indian top and the other wearing a pale yellow T-shirt with a picture of a teddy bear that read "Bear in the Dreaming, Dreaming Bear." Peter and I, on the phone, said, "We have to choose her."

I woke up in the night with the feeling that I was floating above myself. Not like an angel, but like a scientist, studying the strange specimen below. I used to be a perfectly normal woman and before that a perfectly normal girl. My life had been unremarkable. When friends of mine had started blogs, I had tried to think of even one thing I could write about my existence. But loneliness had worked its way into my fibers and altered me and now I was about to start timing my menstrual cycle with a woman on the other side of the globe. In two months I would fly to India with a man whom I loved in terms I could not explain and get a room in the only hotel with air-conditioning. We would go to the clinic where I would be given more hormone injections so that my ovaries bloomed with eggs and he would be given a magazine filled with naked women—*Indian or American?* I wondered—but take from his bag one he had brought himself of naked men, and leave his specimen in the little cup. In a petri dish, our futures would be hitched up like a square knot, a bind that was microscopic and yet so tremendous that it would tie us together for the rest of our lives. Outside my window, the sun was just a hint in the sky. If I wanted a baby, there was a planet of white-coated scientists together with the lush, young wombs of poorer women. All I had to do was travel there.

PETER CALLED TO SAY that he had to come to San Francisco to see his dying grandmother.

"You can say no," he told me, "but I was thinking of asking a favor." I wished the silence on the phone was cracklier, more animated. "She has Alzheimer's. She does not remember what has or has not happened."

"OK?"

"Would you be my wife for the day? Would you pretend that?"

I touched my ring finger and I could almost feel Peter slide a gold band onto it, the loop that meant forever.

Peter's hair was longer than when I had seen him last. He looked younger, more like the boy I had made out with in college. We half hugged. "Thanks for doing this," he said, and handed me a red gummy bear.

In the car, we made up the story of our marriage. We said that we had never broken up after college. "Have we lived in LA the whole time?" he asked.

"No, we spent a year teaching English in Poland," I told him. "And we saved money and then traveled across Siberia. By train. In winter."

"Yes. And we spent a few nights in a hotel that was painted pink and did nothing but eat potatoes and drink vodka. No one spoke English except one couple we met at the bar. He was an arm-wrestling coach and she was a math teacher." I laughed.

"Oh, yeah. Vlad and Natasha. They had four kids, but she was still super-hot."

"But then my mom died, so we came home." Both of us were silent. I had met Peter's mother in real life, in college. I really had sat at her kitchen table and eaten a salad just picked from the garden. Peter and I had broken up the next year, and no one goes to visit their ex-boyfriend's parents. Good people, people you truly like, get shelved that way. You inherit them for a while, but they are not yours.

"Your mom was lovely," I said.

"I wish you had been at the funeral."

"Really?" I asked.

"You were the only college friend who met her. The older I get the harder it is to remember her like she was real. She's gotten foggy. It's like I'm losing her again."

"If we have a baby, your mother will be part of him or her. I bet you'll be able to see her."

Peter opened his window. "This fog," he said, "it feels like being rinsed off."

At the nursing home he took my hand and we walked down the hallway, fake-husband and fake-wife, there to offer comfort to an old woman who would remember whatever we told her, and then forget it again the moment we turned around to go.

The tag by the door read "Lilian Drier, 92, Dementia." So that was what it came to—you live almost a hundred years and the only things left to report are your name and your disorder. Inside, Lilian was brightly lit, her cheeks flushed as if she had just come in from a winter wind. "Hi,

Grandma," Peter said. He kissed her on both her cheeks. She looked past him to me with all the recognition of someone who has come home after a long absence. "Sweetheart," she said to me, "come here to me."

NEXT DOOR AT GATE 23, passengers waited to go to Beirut. They pulled gummy candies out of their leather handbags, adjusted expensive-looking glasses, spread a wool throw over the sleeping baby. A group of thin men punctuated their words with flicks of unlit cigarettes.

My gate smelled foreign. The Indian men had colorful shirts and gray polyester pants. Body odor rode the air like a surfer. An American family passed in safari clothes.

Peter's flight from LA was delayed and I felt half crazy, alone in this airport on my way to sow the seed of my baby in another woman's body.

I put my head back, listened to a jet engine roar, listened to the final boarding call for Beirut. Here we all were together, all these strangers waiting. By morning, we would be on every corner of the globe. Waking up to cappuccino, chai. I thought of the blond family opening their eyes in Nairobi, everyone a little afraid and a little thrilled to be in such a scary-sounding city. Their high-end tour operator would serve them breakfast and whisk them away, but they would see Africa out the window. And isn't that part of the appeal, anyway? Won't the parents feel proud to be exposing their children to the perils of life below the equator? Shouldn't it make those children feel more grateful for what they have—the rooms of their own, the air-conditioning, the sedan in which everyone gets his or her own booster seat, rather than piling onto a moped with nothing to protect them but a small Jesus charm glinting on the handlebars? It was leaving that made home so sweet.

I LOOKED UP at the television to see a breaking story about an explosion at Cape Canaveral. A rocket bound for the International Space Station had burst into flames. The video played on a loop: spark, flames, smoke. I thought of Sunshine, who I assumed was back home in Florida, completing each stage of her training—medical or spaceship technology or Mars geography—until she could finally, victoriously, leave her own planet for good. The first unmanned rocket with supplies for a habitable settlement on Mars was scheduled for two years out. The first crew was supposed to leave in four. Sunshine would be thirty. I thought of that fixed point, the countdown, the launch, and everything that could change before then. The loves that would be loved or abandoned, the body's secrets—illness, desire—come to light. I thought of the stores of freeze-dried sustenance. The explosion was repeated again on the television screen and the pink-lipped newscaster looked grave.

I saw Peter before he saw me. He walked down the long hallway, a coffee in his hand, looking almost peaceful. He was whatever he was to me—my gay ex, my friend, the father of my dreamchild. "Hey, Mama," he said when he got close. He patted my belly. "Feeling anything kick?"

"Not funny," I said. But no matter. So much was possible. Here we were, on our way to a life of meaning.

"Are you ready?" Peter asked.

A fat white guy in a cream-colored linen suit sat down in front of us and answered his loudly ringing phone. "Yes," he said, almost shouting. "Andy, it's the best, the very best you can get." Everyone at the gate stared at him. He looked not at Peter and me but through us, like we were an incidental geographic feature on his horizon. "Andy, Andy, Andy," he said at high volume, "the chrono-layers are socketed.

The entire motherboard has astro-filament. It's the most advanced technology to date. With this in your hands you can do *anything*. It's a fucking superpower."

Peter looked at the fat guy and then at me and we laughed. We two made no sense, but no one else made sense either.

Our plane pulled into the gate, its fuselage winked in the sun. The rocket exploded again on television.

"I'm ready," I said.

Suddenly the fat guy looked right at me. He winked. "Baby," he said into the phone, his eyes fixed on me, "Baby, baby, baby. Trust me. You'll never lose a fucking signal again."

Remedy

The neighbor man fixed things himself around the house. From her upstairs window, Summer would see him outside in the morning caulking; uprooting small, unwelcome trees; straightening the tiled path from door to driveway. Unemployed, probably. Fatter than the doctors recommended. Summer, looking on, suspected there was an entire refrigerator in the garage filled with the bullets of beer cans. Ammunition against this lonely, cold New England.

Out at sea: a foghorn from the ferry, headed away. Beneath it, the harbor would be thick with ice chips. A slurry of salty cold. Summer loved the sound of the aging ship cutting through the near-frozen water, pushing it away in a V. When she and Kit went somewhere, which was not often, she stood on deck no matter what kind of wind was blowing.

The neighbor man left his garage with a ladder. He huffed to the roof's edge, clanked the thing up. Stood there a minute, dizzy or admiring the job. As the man climbed the ladder, his jacket and shirt rose up, revealing a thick black pelt beneath. Summer pictured his wife, whom she only ever saw jogging, her head red and exerted, making good time around the town but always ending up at the same old farmhouse with the same cold day ahead of her.

Summer wonders what it feels like for the wife, her face heat-steaming in the winter air, to come up that driveway, the miles she's covered still humming in her foot bones, and to find that man there. He'd be wearing that same red sweatshirt, the same jeans. Does the woman reach her hands up under the cotton to find his familiar, warm hide?

The neighbor man summits the roof, which makes him seem suddenly much smaller. The sloped black expanse, the single body. From his pocket he takes a beer. He reclines on his elbow and drinks. He lies all the way back. Maybe he is seeing the same black gather of crows on the telephone wires that Summer sees, slick as poured tar. Maybe he is noticing the same crack in the clouds, the slice of almost blue. It all goes still. Summer feels painted into this day.

When the man rolls off, he will do so like a cut log. And when he reaches the edge, his arms will go out and the wind will catch in his jacket and he will look winged. The thud of his body on the ground will surprise Summer, not so much because he is far away, but because it will have seemed to her that he might actually fly.

KIT COMES HOME from his job as a high school English teacher with his hands in his hair. It is dark outside already. This time of year, even day is half night. Summer meets him at the door with a hot cup and cookies. She finds a place for her face in his neck and kisses. He says, "I almost came home at lunch for this," and kisses her back. She wants to wait, to tell him only how much she loves him, to let him put his bag down in the place he always puts it, to stand in the refrigerator's glow searching for a salve for this day. She wants to say, "Good day, sweetheart?" and hear the answer. But instead she says, "One of us is going to die first." All those good knots, tied along the lengths of their lives, but one rope is shorter than the other.

That night, she senses collapse. Kit and Summer together are the answer to any question. The only reason for anything. Because? Because otherwise Summer's body is made out of ripped wing-metal, the burned leather of four seats, glass shards disappearing in the snow. She is the smell of fire and the smell of pine forest and the smell of a storm. It's not figurative. Summer is a construction of the disaster that killed her family. Her parents, dead and entwined in the cold, and she walks away with only a scar on her thigh in the shape of South America that has yet to fade.

Kit is a collage, too. His parents went on vacation when he was six, to a Caribbean island so small it didn't have its own name and the sea around, which was vast, swelled into a sudden lightning storm and though the sea itself hardly noticed the change—what is a little more water when all there is is water?—the island went under. Just like that. Below the surface. Kit imagines two versions. In one, his parents sleep through the storm and drown in a dream. In the other, his mother rigs a sail from their tent and they lie across a downed palm tree, set off on the white-blue waves. There's no ending to that story. The sea is shaggy with palmy islands, with non-people-eating natives, with friendly exotic animals. *It's only two lives,* he thinks to himself. *Two lives to save. More impossible things have happened.*

THE NIGHT AFTER the neighbor man dies, Summer and Kit lie stacked in bed, flesh and flesh. The blanket is ancient wool and itchy, but they don't even consider clothes. They need a solution. "I wouldn't love anyone else if you died," Summer says.

"Then why would you stay alive? You're too young for that. It's impractical, and a waste of skin." Summer notes that they could jump off a bridge together, someplace simple or someplace dramatic. "Better," she says. "Whichever one dies first promises to move into the other, like a house." She doesn't know what form the dead take—mist or molecule—but whatever it is should come on in. Get comfortable. It's good enough for tonight, but in the morning this unenforceable solution will leave Summer wanting.

THE VERY TALK of death makes Summer feel symptomatic. Her arm is a little bit sore. She feels an ache in her guts. She takes a pregnancy test, but only one small line appears. Summer looks at the box again, hoping she misread the instructions. That's the mutation expected in this part of life—new cells like a smattering of tiny stars beginning to make their own gravity. If not more life, then her discomfort must be a sign of illness. As if Summer has invented her own ending, she begins to feel that her heart has been replaced by a ticking clock. She begins to feel dug up and corpselike. Every part of Summer is marching toward the end and the world around her is made of germs, which only serve to speed the process along. She is dying, she realizes. Maybe it will take time for her to erode completely, a clay cliff eaten away by salt waves, but it could be soon. It feels, from the inside, like it could be very, very soon.

Summer says to her love, "It's going to be me. I'll be the one to go." Kit only nods and kisses her at the exact center of her forehead.

"OK," he says.

"No. I'm right about this."

What he doesn't understand is the relief she feels. Not knowing is worse than any answer, and Summer wants this the same way she remembers wanting other comforts: sweaters knitted by hand from the wool of rare rabbits, tiny landscape paintings with gold frames, important books she'll never get around to reading.

Summer opens the phone book and looks up "doctor." She makes an appointment with someone whose name sounds like her father's.

BEFORE SHE MET KIT, Summer prayed to die every day. She imagined the ghosts of her parents in a living room with leather couches and bookshelves that required ladders. She imagined that her mother would have plenty of yogurt to eat and her father wouldn't need to bother with food at all. Except the occasional pecan pie, delivered at exactly the right moment, before he even realized he wanted it. There would be a chair for Summer there. A reclining chair, and outside, a garden. Every day with her foster family in the Boston suburbs, she thought of that place, wished for that place.

High school showed up and she started smoking and watched every single meteor shower for four years. She had friends with cars and they'd drive to the top of the mountain, climb onto the roof and let the heavens fall at them. Maybe there were mountain lions nearby, or bears. Maybe there was a mass murderer in the woods—one girl or another always worried about that—but Summer was ready for any of them. She adjusted her flannel shirt and her torn jeans and she asked someone to climb down into the car and turn the radio off, to let night be the only sound. The friends always listened to Summer. Tragedy lends authority, especially with teenagers. There was a whole hierarchy: divorce, absent father, physical abuse, sexual abuse, dead father, dead mother, and then, at the top: dead both. It was the rarest loss, the most terrible, and the sufferer was like a precious gem, pressed by unthinkable forces into shimmering sadness, shimmering beauty.

Summer slept with all the best-looking boys, and even the mean ones were nice to her. She was loveliest naked, white-gold and cold to the touch, and boys found themselves confessing things on fold-out couches, in cars. *My uncle is a car thief. My brother is in jail. My mother drinks alone every night. My sister is a stripper. I had sex with my cousin. I might love her. My grandfather does not recognize me.*

Summer let them talk. She let them build a little nest

of confessions for them to sleep the night in. Down the dark river they floated.

Kit and Summer met a few years later in a bar in Back Bay where they were with other people their own age. It was hot and awful and so loud that everyone heard only their own half of the conversation.

"I love this song!"

"Yes, Jamaica!"

"You look so hot tonight!"

"I've never had one!"

They all smiled and half danced and ordered another round. The bar-goers did not care about verbal communication—they had so much time for that, their long lives, the quiet morning ahead when they'd reconstruct the night, their ears ringing, their tongues thick. And anyway, anything that could be said with your mouth could be said better with your body.

There were Kit and Summer, mashed up in the dark bar with all those other boys and girls in the smell of spilled and swallowed drinks. They each felt misfiled until the bodies shuffled and they ended up face-to-face, and without one single word, without a question, they shook hands and then they kissed.

They woke up in the morning in the same bed and Kit

said, his hand on the pulse of her neck, "I might already love you." He paused. "I own a house on Nantucket. My parents are dead and I got a lot of stuff. It's not tropical, but I have the keys. Do you want to go there and make up for lost time?"

They went with a suitcase each, just clothes and photographs. When Summer had told her roommates that she was leaving to go live on an island with a boy she'd met the night before, the roommates said, "Oh, cool. Do you want to do brunch first?" They made it so easy to leave.

EACH MORNING of that week, Kit gets up before it is light and makes eggs. He puts plenty of butter on his toast and he looks out the window at the place where the neighbor man slipped off the earth. If only that hadn't happened, he thinks, his girl would not have begun to die. As if death were pollen, airborne. He disagrees with her diagnosis, with the idea that she can suddenly be dying of nothing in particular, but Kit believes Summer. That's the whole thing of it—believing each other is what makes living feel real. If he were to question it, to question her—he can't even think down that perilous path before his valves tighten.

He goes upstairs where his love sleeps on, the blanket pulled up to her chin, hair reaching out like sun-seeking vines. If the neighbor man had stayed on his roof, finished his beer, mended the hole he'd climbed there for, maybe the trillions of cells in Summer's young body would have continued their perfect, coordinated churn. Blood rivering through her, oxygen. The papery folds of lungs, globes of organs. "Forget everything you've seen," Kit whispers to his sleeping love. "You are perfect."

It becomes the method. Tell Summer's body over and again how good it is, how healthy, how undying. Summer thinks it's sweet, how her boy lies to her guts, her thrumming heart. As if lying can make it true. Summer gets in the shower and Kit pulls the curtain back to watch, says, "God, you are beautiful. And so healthy right now." She makes a pot of beans and Kit says, "Look at that strong body of yours. Keep cooking." He buys her lots of ingredients and makes requests for complicated dishes, which she executes perfectly. Evidence of how strong she must be, how present tense, how very here. It feels good. It's a help. But they can only eat so much, and soon, when Kit comes home from work and stands in the refrigerator's glow, he is looking at a wall of leftovers. Half a cake, half a pie, half a roast duck, a leg of lamb, homemade cheeses. Ants have discovered the bread loaves on the counter, poured their thankful black bodies across the crust.

THEY GO TO the doctor Summer found in the phone book. He is lying on the exam table when they arrive, his arm draped across his forehead like he's playing dead. "Sorry," Kit says. "Do you want us to come back later?" The doctor, big and pale, has his shirt open a button and gray chest hair tufts out. He stands up and rubs his eyes, takes a cleansing breath. "You're here," he says, seeming surprised.

Summer does not feel sick today, just as she did not feel sick the days before. She feels good and true and awake after a strong cup of tea. Maybe she's sleepier than she used to be, before she was dying. Maybe it hurts more than it used to to think of the tragedies of the world—the car bomb in the city that doesn't expect that kind of thing and the car bomb in the city that does. The woman who carefully swaddled her baby in a hand-knit blanket and left him at the door of a fire station. The orphans, tens of thousands, who feel around the bed for each other's feet in the dark. *Is that a symptom?* Summer wonders. *Being punched in the heart by the world?*

The doctor presses the cool disc to Summer's chest and listens for a long time, like he needs to hear the whole piece of music, the sonata, all three movements, before he can say anything. In the corner, a stick of incense sends a thin gray spiral up into the room. Above it hangs a piece of silk with the Indian elephant god reaching out. Summer tries to keep her breathing in order. Kit studies his love there on the doctor's nap-wrinkled table. Her ankles are narrow as a child's and her feet hang like ornaments. He wants to merge with her, to entwine.

"Yes," the doctor says.

"Yes, what?" Kit asks.

"Dying," he says. "Every day is a gift."

If Summer's parents, or Kit's, were still alive, surely they would have insisted that she see another doctor, someone with standard medical training. In a big Atlantic seaboard city where even the jawlines of the residents are authoritative. There are no grown-ups looking in on them. There are no friends. The chamber they are in is a two-person chamber and their voices echo off the sides.

LIKE ALL GOOD REVELATIONS, the idea strikes at night. Summer sits up straight in bed and goes to the window.

She slides it open and crawls onto the sloped roof. It must have rained. She draws a line with her finger across her right wrist. "Right there," she whispers out loud. And she waits a moment, expecting a sign or a signal. Confirmation. The peach trees in the yard reach leaflessly toward her with every one of their knotted fingers. By sunlight, Summer has a good start on her research. They will go someplace else far away. Less regulation, fewer rules. It's good to live in a country that protects you with laws, until the only way to love your love after you die is to give him one of your hands.

KIT WAKES THE COMPUTER up in the morning. An email is still sending, stuck. *Dear Dr. Victamsamphe,* it says. *I'm dying soon. My beloved and I love each other so much that I can't possibly put it into words. I want to be with him wherever he is, touch everything he touches, love everything he loves, even after I'm gone. Which is where you come in. Please, it's the only thing that makes sense. I want you to replace one of his hands with one of mine. If it makes a difference, you could have my love's unused hand—I won't need it for long. Maybe there is an orphan or a man who's been in an accident. At least you could show it to your*

medical students. Anyway, that's your choice. We have money.
I'm serious. Please write back.

KIT LOOKS AT his hands. He imagines that one of them is
his lady-love's and that she is stumped. Kit feels a kink in
his heart. His girl is in the shower, soaping her every inch
of skin. He cannot see the maze of tubes and cavities inside her body. He cannot know what is pumping right and
what is pumping wrong, how each of those slippery organs is tucked against its neighbor and whether something
bad is truly blooming there. Whether, even if her body is
perfect, a truck will lose its brakes, tumble off the road
where Summer is walking. There are storms beginning to
twist in the warm oceans to the south, and maybe they
will whip this way, tearing the houses like paper. The ferry
could sink beneath them; poisoned gases could leak into
the air at any time. The melted ice caps are washing toward them. They're both dying—everyone is. The schedule of death is not made public. Summer is not crazy to
take notice of this.

Love's job is to make a safe place. Not to deny that the
spiny forest exists, but to live hidden inside it, tunneled
into the soft undergrasses.

Dear Summer,

You are lucky to love the way you do. A rare beauty. I would like to help you. Thank you for offering your boyfriend's hand to the orphans, but I'd feel better if I gave it to you.

KIT LOGS OUT of his brand-new account. Does not save settings. He goes into the steam-thick bathroom where his girl is drying off, warm and slow, and he kisses her on the insides of her wrists.

"You're perfect," he says.

She clucks her tongue. "I'm starving."

THE NEXT DAY Summer goes to the lonesome small-town library and reads up. The hand is a near miracle. There are twenty-seven bones: scaphoid, hamate, phalanx. One is called the lunate, which is deeply concave and moonlike. Summer turns her wrists, appreciating for the first time two tiny lunar bodies she has been living with all her life. She learns that this bone has a superior surface and an inferior one, dorsal and palmar surfaces. It articulates laterally with the scaphoid and distally with the capitate.

Also: muscles. The extrinsic muscles, she reads, are so called because the muscle belly is located on the wrist. The muscle belly? She reads the sentence again. She pets the place on her arm where she imagines this to be. The other muscles are intrinsic, and that seems like a nice thing to be. In the picture, the blood vessels look like tree roots, knotting and thickening their earth.

Summer begins to get worried. The surgery, she realizes, is unthinkably complicated. Hand replacements can take fifteen hours. Each blood vessel must join another, each strand of muscle must attach. She imagines a room with white floors and very bright lights and a doctor welding together Kit's wrist and her own hand, two body parts that have touched each other a zillion times, loved each other, met in the dark and in the light, outdoors and in, sweating and freezing cold. And yet they are foreign on the inside. Different bloodstreams, different meat. Rejection is a big complication. Medication is necessary for life.

But it's possible. It's been done. And for reasons less pure, Summer thinks, than love. Summer and Kit get into bed that night and talk about one of his students who got hit in the head with a baseball but seemed to be completely fine until the end of the day when his mother came to get him and he ran from her screaming. Kit says that the mother chased him through the high school maze calling, "I love you, Cody. I love you, I love you," until her son collapsed in exhaustion by the snack machine and she fell over him like a blanket, holding him under her hot breath until he went soft. Kit called the hospital to check on him.

"No news except to the family," the nurse said.

"I was there," Kit said. "I saw it. Doesn't that earn me anything?"

"The news is medium-good," the nurse said. "That's all I can tell you."

Summer remembers the vascular system, that web. She thinks of the mother and son, blood-bound. Summer tucks her hand beneath her love's head, catching him in the net of red, red veins.

KIT CHECKS OUT the very same books Summer has just recently returned. Early in the morning, he responds to her emails as her waiting surgeon. He keeps expecting her to write one day and say, *Never mind—too big, too dangerous.* He tries to gently dissuade her. He tells her the story of an Australian police officer who lost both hands diffusing a bomb and later completed a solo around-the-world motorcycle trip with his transplants. He revved the engine with borrowed hands, braked, came to a stop in a tiny foreign village and found somewhere to sleep, all with borrowed hands. Yet all the time the man could feel that the hands were not his own. They pulled at the ends of his wrists. Their motions were ungentle when the man brushed his hair, smoothed his shirt. He had a wife, and he touched her with his new hands and she took quickening gasps of air and kissed him hard, but in the morning he was mistrustful of her. How could she love someone else's hands so easily? *The man came back to me and demanded that the hands be removed*, Kit wrote. *Let me go, was what he said.*

Summer writes back: *This won't be a problem for us because we aren't foreign to one another. I am more familiar to him than he is to himself.* Then Kit tries to underscore the likelihood of major complications. But Kit does not like the way it feels, telling his love that her idea is bad. They live on a dark, cold island and their families are dead and the seas are rising and this house, the pair of souls within, miraculously matched, is all that's safe. Finally, Kit gives in. It's a story, he figures. All he's doing is nodding while his darling tells a story.

The surgeon takes root in Kit's emails. Kit thinks about him at work and a biography emerges, which he types and sends to Summer. The surgeon did all the necessary preparation when he was very young. Time was generous and elastic. You could wake up at ten and go to class, study, take a break to examine the naked flesh of one of your lovelier classmates, eat something smothered in tomato sauce, read some more and you still had the good night ahead.

For ten years, he studied. Always the top of his class. Against the usual course of things, he grew handsomer and handsomer. His hair thickened and winked with highlights. He felt god-blessed, and plus, he was doing important work fixing what was ruined. The little-girl bicyclist and the old-man driver, meeting in an intersection. Her arm didn't make sense as an arm anymore. His job: give her a life to look forward to.

A misfired gun meets an old woman's side. A bear, hungry after the winter; a hiker who walks too close to her cub. A shark, a surfer.

The surgeon sees the world in terms of dividers. Teeth, claws, chain saws, axes, odd pieces of sharp metal, the spikes on a garden fence, a kitchen knife, a car windshield. He stands as the reuniter. In his hands, repair takes place. Brokenness becomes irrelevant, past tense, superseded.

Summer writes back about her sweetheart, how he found a baby rabbit and brought it inside and kept it alive under a bare lightbulb, how he gives old men his place in line. He's good, she's always known it, but saying it to a stranger makes it feel all the more true. In the surgeon, Summer has found a friend. It's a good feeling to know that Kit is not the only person on earth who cares about her. Kit reads the letters at night when his girl has gone to sleep and he wishes he could thank her.

ON THE NIGHT of the first freeze, Kit wakes up and finds himself sitting on the kitchen floor with a paring knife in his right hand. He drops it fast and examines himself for incisions. On the back of his left hand, just where it joins the wrist, he finds a tiny scratch, thin as a papercut. He presses it, though it isn't bleeding. Kit goes outside and feels the cold air hold him. His breath is a gray cloud, disappearing on contact. The invention—the doctor, the surgery—is here with him. It is part of their home now; it is in them.

SUMMER WORKS UP the courage to tell Kit about her plan. Broadly, she tells him, the surgery goes like so: cut, cut, cut, repair, repair, repair. That's simplified, she explains, but it makes her heart feel easier to think of it that way. So many jobs come down to that—cut, cut, cut, repair, repair, repair. The bones have to be sliced with a small, precise saw. It's a sound she is glad she won't be awake to hear. The veins, they are managed with the most delicate pair of scissors. Though of course they are actually stainless steel, medical, Summer imagines her mother's sewing scissors, shaped like a crane with a beak that opens and closes, wings that separate and fold together. Mother-of-pearl inlay and one bright blue eye.

Probably, Summer explains, there will need to be two surgeons, working in tandem. Hands off, hands on. They'll begin early in the morning and finish well after dark. A thousand tiny cuts, a thousand tiny repairs.

Kit has to act surprised. He says, "I'm not going to forget about you. We don't have to do this." Kit knows that he has this one chance to say no. If he doesn't, he will be doubly complicit, both amputee and surgeon.

"We don't have to do anything. This one I'm asking for. I'm thinking January."

He looks at her. It's a story and he does not refuse.

KIT CHOOSES THE ISLAND for its remoteness, its fringy palms, the color of the sea. He looks at pictures on the internet from other people's vacations. They are tan and their towels are covered in sand and they have coconuts with straws. It looks like a good place to be disappointed. Kit knows that land is actual, crossable, and that in a certain number of travel-hours they will arrive on the other side of the Pacific Ocean and no willing hand surgeon will be there to meet them. He knows that the story will end differently than promised, but he does not know what to do other than keep moving forward. Kit has run through a series of possibilities: find a real doctor to do a real surgery; find a fake doctor to do a fake surgery; or, the fantasy that feels most possible, go somewhere far away where Kit's invented doctor supposedly works, but when they get there it's just a local clinic where no one speaks English, certainly nowhere for a complicated procedure, and the doctor suddenly stops writing back to Summer, but the island is so beautiful, so warm and the water is thick with brightly colored fish and the beach is long and moon-shaped, and Kit and Summer sleep in the jungle and they eat strange fruits and Summer finds that she is satisfied, better. That death recedes into the far future. And their love is bigger than ever before, and they don't go home for months because Kit is rich because his parents were rich and this is an inexpensive country and they can live on the water's edge while the entire winter passes at home, all the storms, all the months of slushy sea, until it thaws there and Kit and Summer return with darkened skin and longer hair and they can open every single window in the house and drag their sarongs out onto the lawn and pretend it's Asia. Somewhere in there, Summer's idea, her need, will drift upward and look small, disappear from sight.

IN THE AIRPORT, Kit and Summer sit near a window holding hands and looking out at the geography of grays before them: tarmac, airplane, sky. The orange-vested flight-control man is the single bright spot.

Summer is not sure Kit believes her plan yet. She suspects that he thinks it is a fantasy. She suspects that his excitement is for a vacation in a nation with spicy foods and good beaches, tremendous golden Buddhas and places where orphaned elephants paint with their trunks. That's fair. His love is dying any day—certainly a vacation is deserved.

Kit is inside of the lie now and can't see out. The invention has its own heartbeat, and it has carried them from their small house on their small island, across to the mainland, to the airport. The actual airport where an actual plane is being loaded with dinner, breakfast, snack, and a stewardess in high heels is arranging tiny Zinfandel bottles in her cart and checking to be sure that there is a safety information card in each seat-back pocket. Kit knows he should have admitted to being part of the world that is not sure what to do with her. But here is the invention carrying them along, here is the gate attendant announcing the first boarding group. Here is the body and here are the wings.

He notices that Summer is breathing sharply and she can't keep her hands still. Of course, he realizes: inside her, the wreck of her parents' plane is a hot cinder. Kit says to her, "This is a big plane. Big planes don't crash."

"If we go down you have to promise that we'll both die. I can't be the only survivor again," she says.

He gives her his pinkie to swear by.

THERE ARE WIND-BLOWN WHITE CURTAINS in their hut and a squat toilet and the sand is bright gold outside, and the sea is an almost unimaginable shade. It makes Summer's stomach hurt to look at a blue that blue. Summer and Kit fall into that water, and it catches them, warm. A large gold dog paddles out to them like they need saving and

Summer puts her arms out and lets the dog hug her, scratching, trying to keep everyone afloat. "Sweetheart," Kit says. "Do we need to worry about rabies?"

Summer, already dying, is free from worry now, she says. The stray dog licks her face and looks proud even though Summer is doing all the swimming. When she comes out, her white legs are striped with scratches.

THERE IS NO WHITE SHINE to the clinic floor, no humming lights, no gurneys or nurses in comfort-clogs. There is no waiting room with magazines and fake plants or real ones. There is not even a door. Kit and Summer walk out of the jungle and up three concrete stairs into a tiled room. A fan stirs the air and a young girl sits at a wooden desk with a stack of paper and pens. She smiles at them and says, "Please, your shoes." At the doorway, Summer notices a line of sandals.

"Shoes off?" Kit asks.

She nods.

Barefootedness felt good on the beach, exotic in the restaurant, upsetting in a hospital.

"Is this the right place?" Kit whispers, acting. Summer

looks around and cannot tell. She takes his hand. They watch a door open and a mother walks out holding a baby. The mother wears a T-shirt that reads "Beautiful Today!" It has a cartoon of a cat with a mouse in its jaw. The baby stretches one tiny arm out and opens her hand like something good is going to fall into it.

A small man walks out after them and comes to stand before Kit and Summer. He, too, is shoeless. They cannot tell how old he is—a trick of this continent. Skin here does not record time's passage in the same way. Sun and wind and years slip right over.

"Hello," he says, putting his hands together and bowing slightly.

In the emails, Summer had noted an education, certainly Western. Good grammar. This doctor is foreign. "We're here for the hand transplant," Summer says. She draws a line on her left wrist. "It's so that I can go everywhere with him. Which sounds crazy when you say it, but not crazy when you think it." Her face is hot and blooded.

"Yes, yes," the doctor says.

"Yes?" Kit asks.

The doctor takes Summer's hands and holds them in his own, which are unbearably soft. An American man would be shy to touch anyone with hands that soft. He studies her pinkie, feeling each bone, pressing her nail and watching it whiten. "Very good," he says.

Next he takes Kit's hand, rolls the fingers back and forth, bends the knuckles and straightens them. Kit, too, notes the softness of the man's skin. He notices a ring on his finger. A woman loves this man, lives in a house with him, trusts her children to him, spends long, dark hours with him beside her.

"Bones are challenge."

"Oh," says Summer.

"Oh?" Kit looks at the man and tries to ask him with his eyes what he means. A crossing of wires, he tells himself. No one understands what anyone else is saying.

Summer notices that all the light is natural, tinted green by the jungle outside. There is not a bulb in the place. Summer worries then about power, about the necessary machinery for keeping a body alive under surgical stress. "Do you have machines?" Summer asks. The doctor taps his skull and smiles. She says, "No. Something to make definite of breathing?" Why, she wonders, does she have the instinct to speak bad English, in hopes of being understood? The doctor comes close to Summer and cups his ear around her mouth. "Breathing," he says. "Same, same."

The doctor provides the couple with a series of pills. Kit tries to understand if these are herbs or vitamins or drugs, but the answer to every question is a welcoming smile. "You feel better. Thank you," the doctor says. "Come back Monday."

WHY THE OTHER WHITE PEOPLE are here: to put on scuba gear and watch brightly colored fish deep below the surface of the clear, clear sea is the first reason. The second is to celebrate the moon. Probably the moon is an excuse to wear less clothing than is usually considered reasonable, and to dance as a pack or a tribe or a flock and spin fire-balls above their heads so fast that they draw lines of orange in the darkness, and also the point is to swallow pills and smoke whatever comes around and, if they last long enough, to become even nakeder and pair up, get some of that soft sand in awkward places. Toward the end, when the sun has started to rise again, that's when the people on the beach most appreciate the moon. Enough light to see by, enough dark to hide.

Kit and Summer do not want to dance all night with other people their age who have traveled far to make bad decisions while barefoot. They do, however, want to watch from a distance, at least for a while. The restaurant at the resort at the top of the hill has a good view of the beach, is open late and is supposed to have good fish. You choose your dinner alive, and they smash the skull for you on the spot. The woman at their guesthouse says she'll call them a taxi, but Kit looks up and he sees the resort right there above them. "We'll walk," Kit says.

Bat wings sound different than bird wings. The leather of them slaps at the air. The jungle is thick and ragged with life. It feels like the trees are growing right this minute, adding new inches as Kit and Summer try to keep a path beneath. Rocks and bats and trees, and the small pocket flashlight is not enough to see by. Summer slips down a hill and her skirt comes up to allow a big bruise on her thigh. They arrive at a cliff, not a resort. Below them is the sea, not blue; at this hour, the sea is white.

They stay on the cliff's edge recovering from the hike. The sea makes a good song to rest to. The bass from the full-moon party reaches them faintly and they think of all those bodies moving together in the white light. Kit makes up a song and takes out some tamarind candies, which they share. They are hungry, but they do not want to risk the walk back until daylight. They'll stay the night. At least here they can see where they are. At least here they know where the edge is. "We should put something on your bruise," Kit says. Having no salve, he spits in his hand. "This will help," he says, sweeping it across her leg. "This will heal."

FOR SUMMER, it becomes obvious she and her sweetheart are not great at organizing hand transplants. They are good at swimming and eating fish lunches and they found their way out of the jungle eventually, bravely. Her boy is so kind and helps teenagers get better at writing and he reads in the morning and he has a predictable breakfast order and no parents either—he's perfect. But he's not the man for this job just as she is not the woman for it. Maybe they got the address wrong. She has written to the surgeon every day, but he has stopped responding. She worries about him, because he is so reliable and, therefore, must be injured. Maybe the very fancy hospital was in Bangkok, where all the foreign ladies go to get plastic surgery cheaper and with discretion. The doctors there have all gone to Stanford and Harvard. That's where the famous hand-guy is. She imagines that he has a collection of little moon bones on his windowsill and a Thai wife whose strange culture and luscious hair do not distract him from taking care of her like a full and complete woman, an equal, and they have three little mixed babies and another on the way and he's working on a book about hands, which is really a love letter to what he thinks is the most magnificent invention the body has ever invented, not to mention the fact that the hands are indispensable for all other human inventions. Within this book there is a chapter, still just notes, about Summer and Kit and the beautiful story still to unfold of their joined bodies, of the ways they will hold each other and care for each other with hands that are not their own. Summer worries about the doctor and his unwritten book, the chapter he won't be able to complete without her.

She thinks of him, cutting and repairing bones and veins and muscles. She thinks of him enabling so much work for the bearers of these hands: hammering, hugging, winding the watch, flipping the egg, dialing up the parents, turning the key to drive home, washing the child's hair, unbuttoning the wife's blouse, twitching in sleep, writing the letter to say good-bye.

This island is no place for major surgery. Summer writes a note about needing a walk, leaves her napping darling on the bed. It's the first time she's been alone in this foreign nation, and it surprises her how different it is. She feels skinned, permeable, a magnet for disease and danger.

One of those full-moon dancers could be asleep in the bushes, still drugged and rabid and terrible and hungry for just the kind of ankles the girl possesses. Plus: wet and warm places are snake hangouts, and who knows how to tell the venomous ones from the non-. She hears various rustles and moves to the center of the road where the soft red dirt has gathered in a ridge between tire tracks. Her feet turn color and so do her sandals. If only the birds would quit alighting on branches and looking at her like they are ready to pick her clean.

Summer takes her shoes off and waits for the doctor, whose low voice she hears in one of the rooms. A little boy comes out with a fresh bandage on his foot. His mother has an envelope Summer knows contains medicine. Everyone here has been taken care of, whatever the wound was is clean now, ointmented, covered. The woman and her child will go home and report the accident and the happy ending to the boy's father.

"Shark bite," the doctor says to Summer.

She thinks of all the swimming they've been doing. She thinks of the morsel of a leg. She thinks of the beach-ful of orphan dogs in the shallows.

"Kidding. Jokes," the doctor says. "No sharks here! Your country is sharks. He step on nail."

"Don't cut our hands off," Summer says. "Make up an excuse. Let my boyfriend down easy."

"Feel better?"

"Do you understand?"

The doctor is already walking away. "Watch out for shark!" He laughs. "See you Monday."

THE PLAN WAS DUMB, Kit knows that now. All this distance, but you drag your same old bones, your same old brain with you. Summer has not forgotten why they came here.

So he goes to the doctor for a talk. The road is dusty and he admires the birds along his path. It smells like tea here, and he could eat the good fruits for the rest of his life and hardly anything else would be needed.

"Look," he says when he gets there. "I don't know what's going on here." Kit and the doctor are standing in the hallway, which is dark, and there is a rusted scale and a bag of laundry hanging on a hook.

"Thailand is holiday. You should not spend all of time at my office."

"I lied to my girlfriend, but I did it to be nice. We don't

want hand surgery. Please do not give us hand surgery, is what I'm saying."

"You are not married?"

"No."

"Why wait? It's better."

"She might be dying. She doesn't want to weigh my life down. What will you say about the surgery? That there were technical problems?"

"Try foot massage on beach. Try fresh coconut. Elephants for bathing are here. Eat first thing. Some people prefer suntan and dance music. Quiet OK, too. See you Monday. I'll take good care." The doctor closes himself into a room. Kit puts his shoes on. He hadn't missed them.

THE HOTEL HAS a brochure for deep-sea diving that advertises "an available friendly of small fishes."

"It's irresistible," Summer says. "Meaning we can't resist it." They have to go underwater with someone since they don't know how. First, some information and a quiz, and a medical questionnaire. Summer sees this and gets nervous, already trying to decide if she will lie or not. She wants the available friendly, needs it even. She scans:

pregnancy, head cold, history of heart attack, lung disease, epilepsy, head injury, blackouts. But nothing about general predisposition for death. Summer is relieved. She checks all the no boxes and goes to the mask area to try on masks. Their instructor is a blond from Australia with a high voice from all the oxygen-tank breathing and a neck tattoo of a mermaid twisted up with a serpent. He is responsible for their lives. He says, "Press this to your face and then suck in."

There is a trial swim in shallow water where they learn how to breathe again. It's weird not to know. To have to pull hard to get that bottled air in, and then to blow it out and see the bubbles. They have to learn to clear water from their masks, and they have to learn to give each other air, in case one of them should run out when they are deep down. Summer takes a deep breath and then passes her sucker over to her beloved and watches his chest inflate. She's anxious to get her breather back, even though she has always been able to hold her breath a long time. This is one of the things about herself that she knows and is proud of. Many vacations she spent in the pool daring boys to outdive her. She'd streak across the pool, letting the burn burn her lungs, and when she came up finally, the boys would be panting, holding the edge, questioning her humanness.

They said, "Are you a fish?" but she remembers them calling her a sorcerer mermaid instead.

Kit hands Summer his breather, and she sees him there in the water with her, his eyes magnified in the mask, tiny bubbles escaping his pursed lips. It's terrible not to be able to kiss him then.

Summer borrows a breath from her love.

Descending along the rock wall, they look down and see progressively bigger fish below them. The water gets colder. Kit takes Summer's hand for a minute before they let go to swim better. Coral is fingery and the little fish thread through. They see a turtle and an eel and a giant clam with luminous purple flesh. Kit admires the way a sandy spot looks in the blue cast of the water-light. Some fish nip at the rocks and coral, some fish eat algae off other fish. There is so much alive here that it seems staged. Summer swims at a big school of tiny silvers and they break for her, rejoin after a distance. *The ancestors made a mistake, crawling out onto land,* Kit thinks.

Something glides past. The instructor makes butterfly wings with his hands to explain, but Kit and Summer are not watching him and would not understand his hand language anyway. They know it's a ray. All these creatures are familiar from public-access television. But the ray flies, and Kit and Summer could not have predicted how that would stir them. Water is so much more generous than air; the ray hardly flaps its wings to soar.

THE MORNING ARRIVES. Monday. It came after Sunday and before the Tuesday, and that should not have been a surprise. It had seemed so far away, and the impossibility of that notation: the fact that hand-replacement surgery was written on the particular square of the calendar made the day itself seem unlikely. But here it is, sunny and tired. Summer is up, spearing a slice of banana. She is wearing a white sundress. Kit takes his body through motion after motion. He brushes and washes and combs and dresses. He eats and drinks. See that? Just a day. The ocean is always and already churning. Kit imagines what's underneath— everything is eating, everything is searching.

They hold hands on the walk. Summer tells him that she is grateful for his help, for making this journey. Both of them think of home but neither says the word. No animals cross their path, no snakes. The birds in the trees that morning are ordinary and brown. Neither Kit nor Summer remembers their dreams and both wish they had, wish for a symbol tossed up from the unconscious.

At the steps of the clinic, Kit and Summer kick off their shoes like they're coming home. As if comfort is imminent.

They are led by a woman into a darkened room with a cushioned floor. She gives them each a pair of loose pants and leaves the room. Kit and Summer put on the pants and sit down on the floor. They do not know what is happening to them. Each has asked for a reprieve, is here in hopes that the doctor will relieve them of their own story. Two women enter and kneel beside Kit and Summer, who lie down on their backs. The women climb on top, bend a leg around their own small breathing torsos. The bodies are tangled and bent. The women kneel on thighs, pull limbs up and back. It hurts, for Kit especially. How could someone so small be this crushing? Something strong and herbal is brewing in the room. This is an entirely new smell.

His girl has her eyes closed and her body is making shapes Kit hasn't seen it make before. He has a hard time catching his breath, and in this state, he realizes: it's a massage. We're getting a massage. He has a small woman on his chest, which keeps him from laughing like he wants to. He feels his blood moving through his legs when they are finally released back to the floor. His body, his head feel hot and good.

Kit risks a joke. "This surgery is nice."

"Next time let's switch legs."

Summer hears her beloved laugh. She wants to thank the doctor for this day, for these women who are crawling over the two of them and pressing joint to joint. The hotel has been recommending a massage every day. "No pain, no gain," the waiter told them, pleased to know this Americanism. "Massage fix every problem."

Kits says, "Let's get married. That's what other people our age do when they feel this way."

The women place little warm steamed bundles of herbs along Kit's and Summer's bodies. The smell is delicious and nauseating at the same time. The women stretch Kit and Summer back into their normal shapes and then leave. The room is steamy and dark and this is what relief feels like. Kit reaches over and holds on to Summer's thumb. It is not long before Kit and Summer fall asleep.

SUMMER WAKES UP FIRST. She can't find her balance in the room. She can see her love asleep next to her, his face this far away from where she's used to seeing it. He's beautiful—she should tell him this more. A memory floats in: she is a kid and she still has parents. They're out for ice cream and Summer is sucking the gum squares out of her cone and spitting them onto a napkin. She always got bubblegum ice cream even though it was not the best flavor because you got two desserts in one. The bargainer in her had to make this choice. Her tongue was blue, she knew because she stuck it out and cross-eyed to see it. Her mother was saying something about a dog and her father was saying something about a roofer. A group of crazy people came in, each with his or her own strangeness. One was stooped and was hook-armed with a very short woman who limped. One was wearing too many shades of purple. One had the eyes that made it clear what her disorder was, and she carried a bright pink purse. Summer looked for the uncrazy person in the group, the one who was tending, leading, herding, but she couldn't figure out who it was. Someone needed to be normal and adult, but no one looked it. Summer was worried for the crazies. She told her parents her concern and they both laughed at her. "She's so conscientious," her mother said, like this was an adorable but silly characteristic they hoped their daughter would grow out of. Like wanting to dance ballet, ride a painted pony, wear wide-hooped dresses. It was impractical to be the person she was. Better to grow a shell, to stop seeing so much. Summer ate her gums, one by one, all their color sucked off already, her mouth too full. So much spit. She had to concentrate to keep from gagging.

Summer picks up her hand to scratch her nose but she gets a big white bundle instead. Her hand is fatly gauzed. Like it's been through something. Like an accident. Summer looks to her love and he also has a wrapped hand. She shakes her head around to wake it up. She almost shakes him, almost reaches out with her white mitt, but he's too lovely, too asleep. Summer digs the end out of the gauze and begins to unwrap. There are many turns, and she feels the pressure release as she goes. She is impatient at the same time that she does not want to see what is inside. She imagines unwrapping her darling's hand. She imagines blood. She imagines meat.

Round and round, and finally she sees skin. She can't tell if it's her own because it is so swollen. Waterlogged. This hand looks twice the size of the one she used to carry around on the end of her arm. And at the wrist: a bracelet of stitches. X X X X. It is the way she would have sewn something, not knowing how to sew. Beneath, there is a clean cut. It is beautiful, the cut. The cut is absolutely perfect.

The

Lonesome

Flats

Club Zeus

When Zeus knocked up Leto and Hera found out about it, she forbade the slutty girlfriend from birthing her twin babies on land. Leto rowed the seas until she finally settled on a floating island, which the resort where I'm working claims as our own spit of land, and where I am six weeks into an eight-week summer job before I return to the United States for my last year of high school. There are ruins in the cliffs above the resort, grand columned things in honor of Leto, goddess of motherhood, but here at Club Zeus, we choose to commemorate all those gods and goddesses differently—not that we don't have columns. We have plenty. We commemorate instead with a statue of a big-titted woman in the middle of the huge pool. We commemorate with a make-out pad full of pillows floating in the bay and held up by concrete swans called "Delos," after the island where Leto gave birth to Apollo and Artemis. Mostly we commemorate with as many beverages as you can suck back.

Our guests are Russians and Brits who are fat and white when they arrive and fatter and red when they leave six nights, seven days later. Most of the staff is Ukrainian, but I'm from California. My job is to be the Wizened Storyteller. I wear a distressed robe, rope sandals and a fake beard. I sit in a hut all day and tell Greek myths to whoever comes in. It's kids in the morning, almost exclusively. The afternoon hour is a mixed bag of people who have been in the sun too long, people who have been at Club Zeus too long in general and have exhausted all the other activities, and more kids. Some people just nap. At night I get drunks.

I can tell whatever story I want, so I tailor it to my audience. The drunks get the sexier stories and violence: Odysseus trapped on Calypso's island; Odysseus stabbing the giant, dumb Cyclops in his big eye; the sirens. They tip very well if things get hot or bloody. At the end of the hour I pass around a burlap satchel, hoping that guests will drop in some of their Leto Liras, which they can use for any of the extra-cost items, like fake tattoos or sunscreen rubdowns by the roving belly dancers, and which I will trade in for postage stamps, gum and phone cards.

I came here to escape but so far the pleasure has eluded me.

MY ROUTE TO Club Zeus began with my mother's recent midlife swan dive into the pool of Faith. When she discovered spirituality her whole person sprouted as if there had been nothing there before. As if she had been an empty suitcase, waiting to be packed. I was fifteen.

I had never noticed anything about our home's furnishings until they were replaced: a flowered sofa was traded for a low Indonesian bench with throw pillows; white curtains were given away for brightly colored ones. The kitchen counter became populated with an army of spice jars: star anise, cumin, coriander, fenugreek, sumac, saffron. Mom purchased a meditation cushion and various beads to slip mindfully through her fingers. She wanted her awakening to be inclusive, all-encompassing, so there were rosary beads as well as Hindu prayer beads. She had a book of Sufi stories on top of a book of Zen koans. Saint Francis, his arms beleaguered with birds, looked down upon a singing crystal bowl meant to cleanse the soul. My mother was happy. This cocktail of religions calmed her loneliness as if by prescription.

Before this, Mom had been normal—the same hair and makeup as all the other moms, the same clothes, the mid-forties divorce, stucco fake-fancy house, ambient depression. She had the same three to five glasses of white wine at dinner, the stream of dates with tanned faces and yachts and shitty work hours and insufficient capacities for commitment. This is what it is to grow up in white Orange County; variation is a nonexistent principle.

I did the taking-care-of in our house. I was the one to scramble the eggs and clean the hair out of the drain and Mom was grateful, always grateful. She told me every day that I would grow up to be the kind of man who knew how to treat a woman, that I would be the one good specimen in a state full of assholes. I was happy because I was needed.

Then an unreasonably good-looking blond guy with orange robes and a necklace of marigolds rented what used to be an ice cream shop and hung fabric on the walls and an Open sign on the door and pretty soon Mom started going for morning meditation and then afternoon meditation and then evening meditation and then she went to church, too, and we lit candles on Friday nights and ate challah and she did sage purification ceremonies and got a guy who said he was Cherokee to put a sweat lodge in our backyard. And Mom was suddenly able to take care of herself. She did the dishes, she cooked, she swept the floors. She had been saved and I had been made obsolete.

The deeper Mom went into her spiritual seas, the lonelier I got. One day in November of my junior year, in my fifth semester of the washboard scrape of high school, the geography teacher told us that high school is the stepping stone to college and college is the stepping stone to a good job and a good job is the stepping stone to wealth and isn't that the point of life, isn't that the great dream? It was clear to me that what high school really is is a holding pen: we were too young to be trusted and too old to be cute. The teacher unfurled a map of the United States and opened a box of red-headed pins, which he would press to our dreamed-of college towns. "University of Kansas," said Ethan Peters and the teacher pinned and said, "Lawrence. Lovely town."

"Harvard," said Jessica Stride, who was pretty enough to risk being smart, and the teacher stabbed Cambridge. Everyone spouted their list of reach schools and safety schools. They were believers. They were on the path.

The teacher came to me and I stared at that map and all I could see was the Pacific. All I could see was the edge, a place to leap off and escape, and it struck me, bricklike. All that ocean, all that land, the entire rolling globe, and I just beat a path from my unremarkable front door to this yellow-walled school, gum stuck under every desk, so that I can go somewhere in-state so that I can get a job so that I can raise my kids to do the same? The best we can hope for, the very utmost dream, is to be naked with someone our own age or a little older and muck around with them in the dark? And I thought: *The ocean, the whole entire ocean is right there, walking distance from where I sit.* That day was the day of open eyes, of open roads, and my map included everywhere, just everywhere.

"I have to go to the bathroom," I said.

From point A, which was Room 203 of Newport High School, there was a very obvious path: Coast Highway, Bayshore, stop for a few sandwiches to hold me for a day or two and as much cash I could withdraw, across the bridge to the little cottage-riddled island, wade into the bay to the most seaworthy-looking dinghy I could find, oars in oarlocks, and out. The destination hardly mattered— there were other cities, other towns, islands a few miles off- shore, another country not far south—what mattered was the departure.

I rowed past the gigantic houses with their columns and statues, the big as-if of them. I rowed past sea lions fatted out on the decks of yachts despite the netting the owners had installed. The yachts bowed waterward under all that amphibious weight. I glanced over my shoulder to keep a straight path, then turned and rowed hard.

Within fifteen minutes a police boat zipped in, flipped its lights on. I looked at my sandwiches in the hull, mayon- naise yellowing against the plastic, and I stopped dipping the oars. My big world shrank back down to the size of a postcard.

The arrest was a surprise. I had never done anything bad or wrong, had always associated police uniforms with the Fourth of July parade. They were nice to me, sort of, not mean anyway. No handcuffs, but they put me in the back of their car and read me my rights and the jail cell smelled like microwave popcorn and wet concrete. I thought, *Shit. Oh, well.* But still: *Shit.* My hope turned pocket-sized, and then I couldn't even find it anymore. The warm feeling that had filled my chest, the feeling that maybe I would live a whole life after all, had cooled to ash.

My mother brought me a Zuni fetish when she bailed me out. It was a little beaver the size of a fingernail, carved out of jasper. It had a tiny real stick in its mouth. "Because you are so industrious," she said. "Don't stop being that way." She never asked me why I stole the boat or where I thought I was going. It was as if she already knew, had waited for this day to come, as if she had done it once, too. At home, she made me a sandwich since mine had all been confiscated. It was dark by then, and we sat at the table together. She drowned and saved her tea bag over and over.

"You want to go somewhere?" she asked.

"God, yes."

"OK." So, as a gift for the first time I had ever gotten in trouble—and that's just how my mother put it—she would send me to Turkey for the summer. She had a friend who had an aunt who had a room to rent and they were sure they could find me a summer job. I promised to finish the school year, not to try to run away, not to steal anything. She promised to find me the keys out of Orange County.

———

FLYING INTO the quaint coastal town made me sick in two ways: the choppy air rolled the plane back and forth, and the color of the sea was so rich it almost ached. The land was pine-scrubby and dry, and I could make out wooden ships floating on the water.

My mother's friend's old auntie lived in a little wooden house at the edge of town, which I walked to wearing my backpack, following a hand-drawn map. Jet lag felt like a wool coat I couldn't take off. I was sweating and hungry and overjoyed. The old woman met me at her iron gate, which had been devoured by bougainvillea. She showed me my room—a single bed, a dresser—and then sat me down in the kitchen and poured me a cup of deep red-brown tea in a delicate tulip-shaped glass. She put out a plate of sliced tomatoes, cucumbers, apricots, and a piece of crumbly white cheese along with a basket of baguette slices and a jar of sour cherry jam. It was the best meal I had eaten in my life. I looked up at her, and she looked fuzzy, almost not real, like a half ghost. "What *time* is it?" I asked, suddenly aware that I had no idea when I was.

I WAS WOKEN a few hours later by an announcement over loudspeakers, saying what, I did not know. I joined the old woman on her small porch, and she made me another cup of tea, the second of ten thousand I would drink in the coming weeks. The tiny deck looked out over first the cemetery, then the roof of the corner store, then the road, then the harbor. Most people would try to ignore the foreground filled with human remains and enjoy the sea in the distance. The old woman seemed to do the opposite. After they repeated the broadcast on the PA, I asked her what they were saying. I wondered if she spoke more English than she let on because she answered right away. "Some man, he died," she said.

"Do they always announce that?" I asked. She looked at me blankly. Then she trained her eyes on the cemetery again, like a dog waiting for its dinner. By the time the funeral party arrived an hour later, she had made some syrupy pastries and arranged the brightly colored gummies of Turkish delight into a box and pressed her black dress before heading back out to the balcony to observe the grieving.

We watched together. A pack of strays was circling the

sparse crowd. I had been studying up on the myths in preparation for my job and I thought of Hades, god of the underworld, and his three-headed dog. After the coffin was lowered into the rectangular hole the old woman sent me down to the funeral party with the sweets she had prepared. I didn't know who to give them to. I stood, stupid, for a long few minutes before she yelled something in Turkish and one of the older ladies came and took them from me. I said thank you and she patted me on the head. Then, remembering a contraption I had built for my tree house back home, I went inside and rigged up a basket on a string tied to the balcony so that the old woman could lower her offering herself and I could stay safely out of other people's funerals. Her face brightened when I showed it to her.

"How do you pronounce your name?" I asked. I pointed at myself and said, "David." Then I pointed at her with a question mark in my eyes. She made a series of sounds beginning with a *G*, but when I tried to make them back, I spit out an ugly knot. She raised her eyebrows and gave me a look that said, *Do not do that to my name.* So I said, "I'll call you 'Grams.' It's a term of endearment. It's nice."

She gazed out at the cemetery. She must have known which dead got fake flowers and which ones got real.

Which dead got tears and which ones got a guilty kneel in the dirt for a second or two and then a fast exit.

MY FIRST DAY at work was fun because I had never been to an all-inclusive resort and I'd had no idea how absurd it would be. My boss, Emir, was Turkish but spoke good English. He told me I was better-looking than my photo and then slapped me on the back of the head. The second day was exactly the same as the first, and less fun because of it. The third day I felt a small weight in my stomach, as if a stone had buried itself in the soft muck. The rest of the staff was oblivious to me and the summer-camp camaraderie I had hoped for did not surface. I had imagined that my US passport would get me laid, if nothing else. I could lead a foreign girl to think she might marry me and my long American dollars. But my country's mystique seems to have faded. The Ukrainians hang out together in their dorms at night, the Turks go home to their families, and I go back to Grams and sit on the porch, watching over the dead.

For six weeks I have repeated the pattern: tea and bread with Grams, beard and myths in the tent, meals alone in the staff cafeteria, tea with Grams above hundreds of graves, sleep. The only pleasurable part of the day is when I swim in the sea, cold and wine-dark. Each week, from the other side of the world, my mother asks, "Have you been to a mosque yet?" and each week I have not.

I SIT IN the story tent, waiting for customers. I tell one straggler how Cronus, believing he would be overthrown by a son, swallowed his first five children. "How bloody fun," the straggler says in a British drawl. I try to think of something lighter but the only myth that comes to mind is about Hera forbidding all the gods, goddesses and nymphs to allow Leto to give birth on land, forcing the laboring woman to row across the sea for days until she found a rootless, drifting island surrounded by swans.

The straggler falls asleep. My beard is hot and itchy. What kind of escape is this? In two weeks, I will go home with nothing but a handful of odd details to show for my summer. I imagine the other kids coming back from summers spent surfing every day. I imagine Ethan Peters and Jessica Stride lying side by side on his surfboard, floating out past the break, their skin salty and freckled. They'd kiss—they'd have to, it's the perfect teenage moment for kissing. The long casts of their friends' voices would reel them slowly in, but they'd remember the waves rolling under them, their bodies pressed together trying not to tip the board, their warm lips, and paddling back, each using one arm.

Madeleine Reagan is in Italy studying Shakespeare's plays and sketching marble statues with missing anatomy. I imagine a fly landing in those empty penis holes, buzzing around. I already know that Madeleine will come back feeling changed, that she will have had a crush on an American boy in her group who paid no attention to her and that she will have slept with an Italian without meaning to, and that she will be a little carved out by this but also a little proud. It will be a story she continues to tell in college, a small badge of adult credibility. Marcello would be his name, and he will become a conveniently unknowable person, someone she can change depending on her current needs—he can be a tool to make another boy jealous, he can be the partner in sex acts she pretends to have practiced.

Everyone, it seems, will have had a summer that means something. I can already hear the buzz on the first day of school, five hundred teenagers with stories to tell.

And me? I won't know how to explain anything. I spent the summer at an all-inclusive resort on the Turkish coast with a slew of sunburned Ukrainians. I'll have to explain where both Turkey and Ukraine are to everyone, including the teachers. I lived with an old woman above a cemetery, and I ate a lot of olives, I'll say. And I kissed no one. I fell in love with no one. I told Greek myths to people who spent the whole time joking about yanking off my beard. Evidently I have traveled eleven thousand miles and still found a way to fail at my escape.

"MOM," I say into my phone. It is evening and I can hear Grams outside thwacking wet laundry against a pole. I want to convince her to come visit by telling her that we can hop a quick flight to Egypt and see the pyramids. "Honey pie," my mother says. Her voice on the other end sounds falsely close. Right in my ear. "I've been calling all week," I tell her.

"I know you have. I ended up going on a silent retreat at the last minute. I just needed it. It felt so good, it was just, it was wonderful. One of the dharma talks really reminded me of you."

I do not wonder aloud why it didn't remind her enough of me to call back. To remember that I was real, not just the idea of a son but a fleshy body. "Yeah?" I say instead.

"It was about forgiveness. About forgiving yourself. It

was beautiful." She has forgiven herself. It doesn't matter whether I join her or not. I do not mention Egypt.

It rains for three days in a row. There is almost nothing to do indoors at Club Zeus. I am swamped with restless kids and asked to schedule three extra sessions. I'm talking six hours a day in a scratchy old man voice and running out of myths. "Tell one about love," a drunk man says and I tell the one about Hades trapping Persephone in the underworld with a single pomegranate seed. "Tell a better one about love," says the drunk man's wife and I tell her about how Achilles met Queen Penthesilea in battle, how he saw her courage and fell instantly and deeply in love with her at the same moment he delivered the fatal stab to her neck. The couple leaves without tipping.

At my break the rain has quieted for a moment, so I walk out to the water. An older blond woman is lying in the rain in a tiny pink bikini. She is tanning. *This*, I think, *this is commitment.*

Zeus's Kebab Shack has been turned into a playpen with constant belly-dancing contests, indoor bocce ball and trivia. The British tabloids have sold out completely from the newsstand, even at the three-times markup. There are chubby ladies huddled around the hookah bar looking cold in shorts and tank tops, their faces in the papers. "Everybody Thought I Was Pregnant but It Wasn't a Baby—It Was a 22-Pound Cyst!" Emir is making the rounds, as if a little flirtation can distract the women from their ruined holiday. Sudoku grids are being filled in at incredible speed, and the booze is pouring.

And then, after lunch and before the late-afternoon donut rush, someone notices a fat man facedown in the pool. He is bobbing against the topless goddess statue. Five feet of water, right in the middle of the resort, no splash. His countrymen are all around, with oversweet cocktails in plastic cups, angry sunburns beneath their all-access wrist bracelets. The body is gathered by Emir—suddenly serious, suddenly silent—with the help of two leaf-collecting nets. He, the man who isn't anymore, is given a piggyback ride on the shoulders of a solemn Russian giant of a woman. I watch her eyes as she lumbers toward the medical center. His skin is scattered with small moles. Relief at not being the carrier burns off the people who follow her, like steam.

I am standing in front of the story tent, feeling belly-up. My fingers graze the buttons on my phone. I keep patterning the US country code. I calculate the time difference in my head: it's the middle of the night in Orange County, and my mother is too far away to save me.

A woman runs to the pool and stands there, searching. It is the woman I saw tanning in the rain, I realize. Her hair is white-blond and wet and her face is Russian, without question, firm and resolved, as if it has always known that this would come. His wife. She looks straight at me.

"He's dead," she says, before anyone else says the words. What is there to say to a woman whose husband has just drowned in a pool he easily could have stood up in?

"I'm sorry," I say.

She does not blame me or any of the other people who should have been watching. "Thank you. We will also die someday." She reaches behind the bar and takes a huge bottle of vodka, pours a plastic cupful.

The bartender says, "Take the whole thing, please. Take anything you want."

NO ONE DOES any work the rest of the day. We wander around, gathering wet towels or picking up empty cups, but it's just movement for movement's sake. I am thinking about Grams and the cemetery, how she sits on her porch with a fan blowing straight into her face and watches the graves, some dry and hard, some still soft and round, as though a large animal has recently burrowed in and built a nest there. I wonder if they bother to announce the death of a foreigner. Maybe they do so with a little spark of glee— even white people with disposable income can die here, in this place they flock to to snap photos of the blue-black sea, the bay where sunken columns mark the spot where Cleopatra once bathed. They come here to marvel, but sometimes they find out what the people who live here already know: no amount of beauty will keep you alive forever.

I pull my beard down because I'm feeling hot and faint and I don't at this moment care if I get fired. The fat Russian man did not even exist to me this morning. He was one of hundreds of resort guests whom I may or may not have laid eyes on, but now, by afternoon, he is singular, and he will be in my life forever. I will bring him to bed with me tonight, his facedown form floating in the pool of my mind. He will come to my last year of high school, maybe appear in my college essay, will be one of the stories I tell a beautiful girl I have a crush on to make her love me. I'll bring him home with me, give him to my mother to share with me—though it would be kind to spare her, to tell her only the easy stories of sun and sea, of kebabs and soft breads, I will poison her with this death and upset her peace, because sometimes a person deserves company.

I find myself looking at each person who passes and

thinking, "That guy is going to die," and "That woman is going to die," and "That little girl in the buttery pigtails is going to die." I understand Grams's interest in the cemetery, in the underworld. She is there to check the names off a list of everyone in town, as diligent as a scientist proving a hypothesis—even the pretty young thing with the baby, even the woman so old it seemed she might just forget to pass on, even the Imam, even the politician's daughter. She does not tire of the proof. She survives by it, waiting to hear her own name on the loudspeaker, to hover as a ghost on her porch to see her own box lowered into the good earth, to measure, finally, the love she has accrued. I almost look forward to going home tonight and telling her about what I have seen. I imagine being on the receiving end of her offerings—the tulip glass of tea, sugar cubes, sweets.

I think about the dead man and his wife and wonder who is waiting for them in Russia. There must be children, grandchildren even, brothers and sisters, a whole root system beneath that fallen tree. There must be a lot of paperwork involved in transporting a body back home to be buried. Until it is completed, the wife will have to stay in the fake cheer of Club Zeus, trapped on our merry-go-round.

Kids perpetually flinging themselves down the waterslide, men revving the Jet Skis so that the vibration jiggles their aging testicles, women sliding the strings of their bikinis to check on the progress of their bronzing, everyone pouring drinks down their gullets, too much to eat at every meal. This is the last place where a person should have to mourn.

THE POOL HAS to be drained. There is no yellow police tape in Turkey, I guess, but people do not need to be told to stay away. The guests make wide circles to avoid the empty blue hole, which is at the center of the complex and impossible to avoid. They have taken on an animal skittishness; their eyes dart and they take short, nervous steps. The hookah bar near the pool gets no customers; the alcohol bar, equally close, is full.

Fact I now know: when one of your fellow holidaymakers dies in your midst, you do not stop drinking the bottomless drinks. Your wristband is paid up for the whole week; it's only Tuesday and there is no possibility for a refund. You ask for an extra maraschino cherry, raise your plastic glass to the dead man. You admire the female Ukrainian butts all around, perfectly sized and golden brown, the peek of white skin where the thongs shift as the women high-heel saunter. You burn and peel.

THE HIGHER-UPS HAVE asked that everyone stay late in case the police want to question us. I try to call Grams to tell her that I won't be back for dinner, but she does not answer the phone. When the sky finally darkens, I go out to the swan-supported island, hoping I will be alone. In the corner is a statue of Leto, half clothed, holding her newly born twins on a drifting island. They look happy. They are a family and maybe that is enough. They know who they love. I lie on the tile floor listening to the water lob itself into the pilings. Finally, I dial the number.

"Mom," I say, as if I am prompting her to be that person.

"Oh, hi, sweetheart."

When I tell her about the fat man, there is a thick silence. I hope the story hurts her. I want her to share what I am feeling because my pain is part of her job. "Love," she says. "Oh, love." But she sounds proud of me. As though she is congratulating me for achieving a long-held goal.

I try again to capture her, to drag her into my sadness. I say, "He was just floating there. His *dead body* was just floating there."

There is a pause and I think I may have succeeded. Then she tells me, "My friend Ashtar was over today and he saw that picture of you when you were five, with the tractor. He said you have an old soul. You are stronger than you know."

What she means is that I am on my own. What she means is that tragedy is also currency. That enlightenment depends on grief. That love grows in soil that has been tilled. For a moment, I wonder if she planned this whole thing, if she prayed to all her gods not for my safety or for my happiness but for me to be deepened, opened, undone so that I might begin to blossom into my truest self.

The water continues to roll into the pilings. The god of the sea must be hungry and sorry. The pilings are stoic and disinterested. After a long time I fall asleep, and sure enough, the fat man joins me there, lying next to me face-down, as if he is waiting for someone to rub sunscreen onto his big freckled back.

A HANDFUL OF FINGERS are in my hair, waking me. They are thin and curious, and I jerk away. A woman is kneeling beside me. There is enough light to see that it is the dead man's wife. Her face is hollow, as if she is wearing a mask. Beneath, what could she look like? What dark cavern would I find?

"I must love somebody," she says.

"I'm sure you do," I answer, thinking her statement is an existential one.

"No, now." And she falls into me, her lips on mine, suctioned. I try to pull away, to turn, but she has a hold on me that I can't break. I am the dock and she is the snail. The dead man's wife's tongue is in my mouth now, slipping and searching, and then she has rolled on top of me, and the air goes out of my chest. I am just a place, a heat source, and that is enough for her. Keeping my arms pinned to the floor, she kisses up and down my neck, her tongue in my ear is incredibly loud, like a sudden storm. I can still feel the fat man nearby, floating, and I think maybe the woman can feel him, too. Maybe I am him right now, to her.

I notice that I have sustained a small wound for the dead man's wife. Like a paper cut somewhere inside me, sharp-edged and very distinct. It reminds me of when my mother would forget to pick me up at school on time, how I'd stand in the semicircle driveway watching the sun sink and worrying that she was dead or trapped someplace, until her car finally glinted into view and my sadness shifted through relief and into trying to soothe her guilt. "Don't feel bad," I'd say. "It's OK. It's not cold out."

And then I kiss the dead man's wife back. Out of resignation? Out of kindness? Because I felt a flutter somewhere deep? Sensing me agree, she lets my arms go and I wrap her up, feather my fingers over the folds of her neck. Her skin and my skin are as different as paper and rubber. I imagine what I know about the Soviet Union and Siberian prisons and Chernobyl crashing up against the dullness of my life like a battering ram. Bread lines, the KGB and nuclear disaster, the endless sunny emptiness of being a teenager in Orange County—they bust open the frozen-banana-stand summers, the pack of blond children learning to sail, the Ferris wheel handholding, the failed marriages, the less-than-perfect mothers, the kids who return after the first year of college and everything they wear, head to toe, is branded UCSB, Harvard, Texas A&M. Gloriously, my life is torn to shreds by the dead man's wife. None of this is real, says the fucked-up history of her country, her brand-new widowhood. Nothing, it says, has truly ever happened to you.

I kiss the dead man's wife and let my hands go up her shirt, cup the soft egg sack of her breast. It is the wrongness that feels the best, the fact that I cannot justify this night. I am doing someone a disgusting favor, inadvisable in every way. She is doing me a favor, too. A simple physical pleasure rolls through me.

She does not take my clothes off, maybe because she knows my skinny half-grown body would be ruinous to her fantasy. I keep pushing my shirt up and she gently smooths it back down. I have sunk far enough into this warm wrongness to want it to go all the way, for us both to come up gasping at the end, to not even be able to look each other in the eye. I want to walk around for the rest of the week knowing what I've done.

As I am getting ready to dip my hand below the waistband of her denim miniskirt, I hear something shuffle. The dead man's wife sits up, hears what I hear. She pulls her tank top down but not before I see the tanned folds of her stomach in the moonlight. She has the same stretch marks as my mother, a white roadmap on her sides. I remember pulling at my mother's skin, asking her why she was tracked like that. "You did that to me," she told me. "You grew and grew and grew and I had to stretch and stretch and stretch."

Someone appears on the steps nearby. It's my boss. I try to gather myself. The blood leaves my crotch.

"The woman has been calling and calling," Emir says.

"My mother?"

"No, no. Here. Where you are staying."

I think of Grams on her porch, waiting for someone living or someone dead to appear. She was worried—it never occurred to me that she would miss me. I wish I were on the porch with her, looking out over the graves, the night sea just a shadow in the distance.

Neither the widow nor I explain why we are here on this floating island in the sea. Why we are alone. Maybe I'll be fired. It's almost the end anyway. I am leaving in two weeks and Turkey is very far from my home and Grams is old and we are unlikely to ever see each other again. Emir's hair, thick with gel, shines in the moonlight. He gives me a little headshake as if he knows every terrible thing I will ever do. He must be used to bad holiday behavior, but this is of another order.

The widow turns to me and puts her palm on my forehead as if I am sick. She looks at Emir and her eyes are soft. "Good boy," she says, coming to my defense.

I wish that I were younger, that I could feel the feeling of being a child with a person who knows how to take care of me. Out of habit, I close my eyes. Her skin is cool and cooler still is the metal of her wedding band. I imagine its counterpart on the finger of the drowned man, his skin swollen around that bright promise. My mother was right: pain is an enzyme and I am softened. A year from now, when a girl asks me if I've ever been in love, I will lie and tell her no, but only because I will not know how to explain this night. Love, I want to say to the widow, to Emir, love is an island. But when I open my mouth, the words get tangled. It begins to rain again. Emir clears his throat, trying to prompt us all to return to our separate lives. But when I lean into the widow's hand, she holds my head up. Below us: all the world's water.

High Desert

Two thousand years after her people left Jerusalem and eighty years after they left Turkey and fifty years after they left Poland and twenty-nine years after the death of her daughter, the woman walks down the desert road and she feels her body letting go of her.

She is not dying. She is not sick, even. Her body is detaching itself. In fact it is just that her uterus is heavy and falling, but she feels like her body is untying the knots and setting off. The sky is rich blue, clouds puffed, the dirt road dusts her shoes. She looks up at the mountains, the open sky.

The doctor's secretary says to come on in. Each step the woman feels the falling thing. "Get back in there," she whispers. "There is no place else to go, I'm sorry to tell you."

"You aren't dying," the doctor says.

"Yes I am," she tells him. "So are you."

"Ha," he says, "ha."

"Anyway," the woman prompts him.

"It's not a big deal. Your uterus is falling, is all. It's gravity, our old friend."

"What do we do about it?"

"You won't need it, I'm guessing?"

"How many women live in your house?" she asks him.

"Plenty, I guess. How many do we need? One is enough."

THE WOMAN HAD a husband and she had a daughter and they lived on an island in the Caribbean and it's possible to remember that time as good, easily and simply good. There was lobster and sun and the husband worked in a shop and the daughter went to school and every Friday they lit candles and put their hands on the same kind of bread while the rest of the country waited to pray until

Sunday. It was good because it could have gone a different way. Because the parents of the woman and her husband had died and the uncles of the woman and her husband had died and the towns where they had been born were entirely emptied of Jews. But these two did not die and they crossed the ocean when they were still children and they were welcomed to this island and they grew up and met and fell in love and married and worked and had a baby and all they had to do was never look too far east.

But then this daughter, this girl, she went to the beach one day when she was fifteen and she did not come back. Her friends said it was a wave. The sea swallowed her up into its blue blue blue. The sea was hungry, or the gods of the sea were and they never spit the girl back out. There were searches by air and by boat and on land but the woman knew from the moment she heard the news that the girl would not be found. And when she wasn't, the husband swam out, too, and let the sea claim him and the woman took a bag of things and set out to find a desert.

THE DOCTOR'S OFFICE features photographs he took himself of Machu Picchu, Ayers Rock, the Great Wall of China. He is wearing a huge turquoise bracelet and his arms are tan. He sees her looking at the photos and says, "There is nowhere like New Mexico, though. We are so lucky to live here." The woman lives here because it is dry and far above sea level, but she admits that it is beautiful.

"We have two choices," the doctor tells the woman while she lies down, feet in stirrups, legs up, waiting. "We fashion a kind of plug, made to fit you, which pins the uterus back up inside. You come in once a month and I clean the plug and replace it."

"That sounds dreamy. I guess we get a lot of chances to get me in this position."

"Oh, there is no need to feel embarrassed. I do this all day."

"Option two?"

"Option two, we take the thing out. The whole apparatus."

Apparatus, the woman thinks. As if it were rusted screws and oxidized iron.

The woman does not want to go home after her appointment so she takes the bus to the mall. She has no intention of buying anything. Unless there are any deals on practical handbags. She needs no more of these, has not needed more for decades. She has many small, sturdy purses with useful pockets nested in her closet. She does not buy them so much as adopts them.

On sale instead are bright lacy panties. Not cotton like she wears. She holds lime-green thong underwear in her hand. They are 75 percent off, today only. They look fertile to her and she finds herself wanting them, needing them, for the possibility of love more than the love itself. She takes four pairs to the counter.

"OK," the saleslady says, "panties!"

Thinking of sex and fertility and bodies, the woman says, "People are probably having babies today."

"I bet you're right."

"And dying."

"OK," the saleslady says, stuck now in a conversation she was not trained for. "Well, here are your panties. I hope you have fun with your panties. I hope you have a blessed day."

THE WOMAN STANDS on the corner outside the mall and unbuttons her coat. Who knows what time of year it is on a day like this. The problem is not her affliction, which is painless and possible to remedy. The problem is that her body was once a house where her daughter lived. The problem is that the two of them lived there together. The room her daughter occupied, the room where she swam—it's impossible for the woman to forget this fact, that her girl was a swimmer first—has been a silent comfort. All these years she has carried the tiny inland sea her daughter swam in. Thinking of it this way makes it more possible to survive against the real sea with the girl in it.

Three teenage girls approach in short skirts, and though it is a nice day for this time of year, it isn't that nice a day. There is nowhere to go in this town, nothing to do, and the woman feels sorry for these girls who just want to take their young selves out and be seen. The woman studies their faces, just like she has studied every face of every girl in case it is her girl, in case her daughter has found her way home. Her daughter would have been forty-four now, but it is the faces of fifteen-year-olds that the woman always looks at.

"Here, have a pair of panties," the woman says to one of the teenagers as the group passes. The girl does not take the panties. "Please," the woman says, "take them from me. Nothing is wrong with them. Everything is going to be fine."

"Fucking weirdo," says the teenager, and goes on.

People want to buy things, but they do not want things for free. People do not know how to accept a gift.

THE WOMAN GETS on the bus and looks out the window. A purple bruise of a storm darkens twenty miles away and the woman watches it move across the juniper and piñon. She knows she will be able to smell the rain long before it arrives. The old woman looks over a pamphlet given to her by the nurse. On the cover is a pencil-drawn picture, like an art-class sketch, of a naked woman with all her anatomy visible. The person, as these people always are, is standing with her arms a few inches away from her hips, her palms out. She looks like she is waiting to be saved, to be taken up to heaven or to dive from a great distance into a deep sea.

Above her are the words "Your Happy Hysterectomy!" Inside are facts.

One in three women in the United States has a hysterectomy by age 60!

It's the second-most common surgery for women after the C-section!

The hysterectomy can either be completed by making an incision through the abdomen or by going in vaginally!

If it's possible to go in vaginally, the recovery time can be less than two weeks!

Having the uterus removed before menopause has greater side effects!

Ask your doctor about hysterectomy!

The woman puts the brochure down on her lap. The rainstorm is still far away. *What are you so worried about?* she asks her impatient body. *We're Jewish, did you even know that? We don't have a heaven. We have Israel, but it's easy to die there and it's hot. They would like to think that you can get a good bagel, but it isn't true. You helped me make a daughter. I'll always be grateful for that. If there's anything left of her, would you please leave it with me? I hope it works out for you, wherever you're headed.*

THE DAY ITSELF is easy. The woman's neighbor comes with her, waits in the lobby, picks her up at the end and takes her home. The woman goes to sleep. When she wakes up she is foggy with worn-down anesthetic and pain medicine. She looks up and there in the chair beside her bed is her daughter. She is dripping wet, her hair matted and green, her feet slightly webbed.

The woman cannot stand up, so the girl comes over to her and lies down beside her mother, soaking both of them. She smells sweet and reedy and the woman begins to weep and kisses her girl on the forehead. Her skin is warm, still warm, despite all those years in the water. The woman wants to lick her daughter dry.

"When you were a little girl, six years old, I came in and found you sitting on the floor looking at your palms. I remember you were wearing a T-shirt with two cats on it that said 'Sophisti-cat-ed.' I asked you what you were doing and you said you were checking to see if you were a saint. 'A saint?' I asked you. 'I'll get cuts in my hands if I'm a saint,' you told me."

"This is embarrassing," the daughter says.

"But you weren't a saint, you were a fish. How could we have known?"

They lie in the bed for hours, possibly days. They drift off, awaken. No one gets hungry. No one gets thirsty. No one moves.

The room turns gold with evening light—who knows which evening it is—and the woman sits up for the first time and they look around. The brochure from the surgery is on the nightstand. At the daughter's suggestion, they cut the figure out of the picture. The daughter goes to the kitchen, her feet awkward on the floor, slapping and leaving a trail of water, and comes back with a newspaper. She folds it into a three-inch-long boat. She turns the hot water on, leaves it running. She helps her mother into the bathroom and they both sit on the floor.

The daughter places the ship in the water. "Time to go to sea." The bath fills higher.

The thing floats along, bobbing. Right away the newspaper soaks through.

"Did you ever encounter your father? He went in after you."

"There are a lot of ways to take care of someone," the girl says. "He did his best."

"Don't tell me if you suffered. Don't tell me what it was like in the water before you got used to it."

The bath is full to the brim but no one reaches to turn it off. The boat gets lower and the newspaper begins to bloom. The little lady figure is still slick and stiff. She floats on her back, her arms out.

The woman puts her head on her daughter's shoulder. Water begins to spill over the lip of the tub. It is warm and good.

The floor is wet, the bathmat is wet, and the water keeps pouring. The little figure washes over the side of the tub and floats now on the pool gathering on the floor. The mother lies back in the warm wet room and the daughter lies back in the warm wet room and they put their arms out. They grab hands and float.

Heaven

It's his address, the man tells himself, that makes love so difficult—his house is at the junction of the River of Stealing and the Falls of Eternal Despair. The man often imagines how he'd give directions, if anyone would ever come looking. It's left at the Pond of Bowling. If you get to the Pond of Cards and Saloons and Church Lotteries, you've gone too far.

THE MAN FEELS CLEAR that he is only here because land was cheap, cheaper even than on the Lake of Private

Dancing. He's no sinner, he says. The plan is to fix the place up, sell for more than he paid, get into a condo or a loft, stacking washer and dryer, stainless fridge. He sits on the porch looking up at the bright white mountain of Heaven, not at all far away, hovering. He is handsome and sturdy, the kind who profits from his good investments.

THESE SWAMPS ARE feverishly green, saturated earth that can't help but invent a hundred new kinds of vines each year. His is a floating house, tethered to the deepest roots of the vines with fresh ropes. The ropes the man makes from the sinners' old clothes, the relics of their lives, cast out in a last attempt to be forgiven. "What if I throw away everything?" they say, nakeder and nakeder as they go. The man in the floating house doubts that a late decision to abandon one's shirt is enough to get saved. The man shreds the guilty rags quickly because the specificity of them makes him sad. This faded pink-and-gray flannel shirt with a ring in the pocket from thirty years of carrying the same brand of chewing tobacco. Stains on the front from splattered spit-brine. Loneliness.

———

ON A STRANGE BRIGHT DAY, sun where there isn't usually any, a dress catches on a branch. It is red, meant to tie around the waist and be untied by a true-lover and holding it makes the man feel suddenly very far away. He imagines pulling the dress's woman onto the good earth, a vision, her whole self bared and holy and ready, everything unbeautiful washed away. How long it has been since he's touched someone. The man hangs the dress as carefully as if it is the woman's shell. The arms are empty and begging, and the man comes close and wraps them around his body. They are grime-wet, and they stick to his skin. He is held on to.

The Dream

Isles

The Animal Mummies Wish
to Thank the Following

For generous donations in support of their preserva-
tion, the animal mummies wish to thank the Institute
for Unforbidden Geology, the Society for Extreme Egyp-
tology, the Secret Chambers of the Sanctuary of Thoth
Club, and President Hosni Mubarak, who may seem to
have been around a long time, though not from a mummy's point of view. They wish to thank the visitors who
make it to this often-skipped corner of Cairo's Egyptian
Museum, which bears none of the treasure of King Tut's

tomb. And to the British colonial government, without whom the animal mummies might still be at rest, deep in granite tombs, cool and silent.

They would like to thank Hassan Massri of Cairo, Alistair Trembley of London, and Doris and Herbert Friedberg of Scarsdale, New York, for their support of climate-controlled cases to house the animal mummies for the rest of time. The animal mummies will admit they are somewhat surprised that this is what the afterlife has turned out to be: oak and glass cases, Windexed daily; a small room, tile floor, chipping paint; the smell of dust and old wood. Even for the permanently preserved, the future is full of surprises.

The animal mummies wish to thank their mothers—and their fathers, but mostly their mothers. Gauzy now, two thousand years later, they still remember being licked and suckled. The vole mummies remember the feel of their mothers' teeth grazing—painlessly, absentmindedly—across small, tufted cheeks. To be a vole like this, forever, unendingly as the vole mummies are, is to know humility. No one asks to be born a vole. No one dreams of millennia of voledom. The vole mummies would like to thank everyone who, through these drawn-out centuries, has not confused them with moles, muskrats, mice or shrews. They would like it noted that they are proud to have been small enough to hide beneath the bed listening with their soft round ears to the pharaoh and the queen rattling toward a different kind of eternity. In their memories, they are a mighty brigade, moving soundlessly through the kingdom, pawing tubers on the banks of the Nile.

THE SNAKES ASSUME that someone would like to thank *them* for being so easy to enshroud.

THE MUSEUMGOERS WEAR shorts and hats and T-shirts with names of places on them: Kenya, Norway, Hawaii, as if they are trying to communicate their origin to the dumb natives. *We do not care what dirty modern city you sleep in, what sad vacation you once took,* the cat mummies think. Where did the cats come from? Where did they live? At the feet of queens; on the banks of the mighty river. The cats were a million gods. In those days, when a cat died, its family shaved their eyebrows in mourning. If a man killed a cat, whether he meant to or not, he was sentenced to death. Those were days of justice.

———

LAST WEEK, WHEN the squat man in a blue suit clomped up the stairs to their dusty little museum tomb and hung a plaque on the wall stating "The Animal Mummies Wish to Thank the Following," with a list of donors, the cat mummies thought, *Do we? Do we really? Doris and Herbert Friedberg?* Next, they figured, they would be told to bow down to a group of ten-year-olds and their imbecilic drawings of pyramids. *You'll have to find a vole to do that*, the cat mummies snickered. If the cat mummies must be grateful for one thing, it is that they are forever-cats, and not forever-rodents. The cat mummies can think of nothing so embarrassing as that—the great gift a vole gets is, finally, to die. If he is very lucky, his toothy little life comes to an end at the paw of a stealthy feline.

THE NILE CROCODILE mummy would like to thank the egg from which she hatched, though she does not remember such a time. She would like to thank the Nile, for obvious reasons. She would like to thank the ship full of sailors that ran aground, for those lovely thighs and buttery, soft drumsticks, and also for their bracelets and jeweled rings, which she has kept in her great preserved belly since. Life now, and death, are given meaning by the cold weight of those treasures in the center of her lengthy body. The crocodile mummy would not like to thank whoever it was that stitched her jaw shut to keep her from biting in the afterlife. If only she was not staring for all time at the small nugget of a vole, unable to open her giant jaws and clamp the bite-sized creature between her knife-edged teeth. She dreams of meeting the man who mummified her and ever so carefully running a silk thread through his upper and lower lips.

THE BABOON MUMMIES would like to thank their owners for having the foresight to remove the baboons' canine teeth so that they, forgetting their masters' fragility for a moment, could not bite off a little finger and chew on it before the fury of guilt and regret kicked up like a storm.

THE EGGS WISH to thank the idea of life, which has reassured them over the centuries that they were preserved in earnest, not simply because the priests mummified anything they could get their hands on. The eggs have been waiting for three thousand years to find out what they will hatch into. Will they become crocodiles or hens? Surely, when the egg mummies finally crack, it will be a god who has broken them.

GRATITUDE IS NOT what the dog mummies wish to give. Their museum tag explains, "In Abydos, Upper Egypt, dogs were buried in the same area as Women, Archers, and Dwarves." The dog mummies are insulted. Is there some through line, a theme, they do not understand? Once the thin-nosed guardians of young kings, they now find themselves in a permanent state of death, crusty and gawked at. *What an honor*, the dogs snicker. Life, that single luminous moment, would have been enough for the dog mummies. They remember their names: North Wind, The Fifth, and Useless. They remember stalking the night-dark graveyard where the stones were still warm from the day. Caught rats and voles flicked their tails against the dogs' noses. Children moved aside in the market when the dogs passed. When they died, old and tired, full of the memories of the long walk their lives had been, they were ready for that to be the end. So who, then, would the dog mummies like to thank? Each other, because they were a living pack and now they are a pack frozen in time, each with one front leg bent, waiting for the right moment in this eternity to make a run for it.

THERE ARE ALSO bodiless mummies, shaped mostly like cats. Empty spaces, preserved forever. They wish to thank their mothers, though they have none. Instead, the nothing mummies would like to thank the priests who made them, carefully as they did, as if what was inside was sacred. As if to wish for a cat is to create one. Before these priests, they were just cat-shaped gusts of air, invisible. Now, they can almost remember what it might have been like to be alive as such a beast. The voles they would have caught. The golden collars they would have worn. The real cat mummies are filled with bones and a heart. The nothing mummies are filled with prayers written on slips of papyrus, organs of faith. If scientists came and cut them open, the nothing mummies wonder: Would the little piece of hieroglyphed papyrus rolling out be any less beautiful than the dried raisin of a heart? Aren't they not only the container but the prayer itself?

Enshrouded and encased, the animal mummies are trying to be patient. They did not expect the afterlife to be lit with flickering, fluorescent bulbs. Darkened sarcophagi, woven boats rowed across the heavenly river, glimmering, gorgeous night—that was what they thought would be in store after they died and priests washed them with palm wine and pulled white linen tight. Voles imagined their emergence into the next life, a place filled with nuts to paw, holes to hide in, secrets to keep. When the newly mummified eggs dreamed, they could almost feel something inside them begin to peck. But time has no ending and forever meant forever. Someone's fingertips prepared these animals for the farthest of journeys—their noses were stuffed with peppercorns, their bellies with lichen and their eyes were replaced with onions.

THE CAT MUMMIES allow themselves one fantasy: if only there had been no such thing as an archaeologist. To think of the day they were dug up makes the cat mummies sick. Awake for the first time in thousands of years, they peered out, wanting to see, finally, the afterlife. Instead: the inside of a crate, the inside of a canvas tent, and then someone began, with fine-tipped tools, to dissect them. If only they had remained entombed in the cool earth with their kings. *We were not afraid of eternity, of forever,* they think. They would have made the journey to the other side, no matter how long it took. No matter how furiously, how magnificently long.

THE MUSEUM AT NIGHT is tomblike and comforting. Without the lights, without the visitors, without the plaque on the wall, the animal mummies can almost believe they are in their right place. A clay cave. The very center of a pyramid. Maybe, the voles hope, it is not the end. This could be only one of the worlds they must visit before they reach their true destination. Perhaps, the baboons pray, the animal mummies have much to look forward to. This place could be nothing more than a test of their faith. No matter how many disappointing days begin with the hesitant blinking of a fluorescent bulb, there is always another night on the way. The time to dream is plenty. What if, the eggs imagine, they have not yet left the shore, the tossing waves of the Nile are still ahead, and beyond them the true afterlife: kings and queens wait to receive rodents, baboons and cats, their royal arms open, welcoming home their great, delicate slaves.

Do Not Save the Ferocious, Save the Tender

It was dark all the time, and so it was dark when the ship's captain crept into the corner where his young daughter was asleep. It was dark when he carried her out onto the deck and raised her up in the moonlight to better see his claim.

The whole sky turned green with fire. The girl looked up at her father, at his matted beard. He said, "I loved you first." He thought of her nine years, all of them under his care.

"You loved me before you hated me?"

"I loved you before anyone else did. I'll love you after whoever buys you stops." The captain lowered his head and kissed her on the mouth. She smelled like fish oil. She turned away. The sea churned below them and the captain was no less lost. Through the girl's thick clothes, a little bit of human heat escaped.

The girl was young enough to seem alive. He said, "We're lost. We've been lost for weeks. I'll take something good before I die."

The captain kissed her again, mashed at her with his thick tongue.

Yet more sea rolled under them, yet more water.

The girl pulled her head back, looked up at him. From a leather belt she drew a blade, which glinted. It might have been the only clean thing on board. The girl raised the knife and she sliced her father's lips.

BY MORNING the captain's face had begun to blister and rot, and at the very same time, the ship began to blister and rot, as if the man and the bilge were one body. As if he had hot-mouth kissed a hole through the old lumber, straight to the glacial abyss. In a single day, the bottom softened and the craft split open.

Men and women and children and babies and chickens and goats and bricks of butter and yogurt and dried meat and murky vats of alcohol bobbed on the freezing surface for a few breaths before starting the slow, sinking journey to the bottom of the world where the muck-thick gods would welcome them.

TWO MEN, Esa and Paer, were belly-flopped across what wood was left, praying to a thousand different gods. The water was dark and clear and miles deep. There were pieces of ice, dirt-gritty and luminous blue, floating.

The heart tripped and panted with a desire to save; the body knew not to go in after the beloveds. The fearful skin pressed away, onto the shingle, away from the blue. Esa, from the cage of his head, watched three ghosty women disappear below him, their leather coats opening and waving like the skirts of a jellyfish. Their legs, those unkicking tendrils, white as pearls, were sinking treasure. Women's legs in those days were hidden beauty, cloth-covered and unmemorized. A shame, Esa's twirling mind said, a shame to have kept that flesh hidden, seeing how short its time turned out to be. It had been easy to think that arms were for hoisting and hauling, the only fire was a rope burn on the palm.

Paer watched everything go down. He craned over the edge of the raft, his right arm in the water, reaching. Paer gathered a bowl, a man's undershirt, a comb carved from the antler of a reindeer—what an impossible creature that seemed then, land-sturdy and strong-footed on the big, traversable surface of ice and tundra. Paer's arm turned stiff but he did not remove it. When his wife sank below him like he knew she would, he reached for her, touched her ankle but could not grab because his hand had frozen by then.

Esa had seen Paer and his wife together over the months at sea, and it had been unremarkable. She handed him one thing, he handed her another. She slept in the women's quarters, he in the men's. Now, Esa saw that Paer was a body severed from itself. It made no sense for one to exist without the other: there is no such thing as half a heart, still beating. Esa's throat stinging with salt, he thought of the gods waiting to catch her. The giant man and his thousand daughters, their pots full of sweet liquor, gathering bodies to dance with in the everlasting celebration of death and cold and water and darkness.

Paer put his face in the water, but Esa pulled it out by the hair and made him drink the air. *Where, where, where,* Esa sang, somewhere in the foggy forest of his mind, *drift, drift, drift.*

THE CAPTAIN, on another shingle, turned himself over and looked up instead of down. His ship, his crew, his daughter went deeper and deeper below him. He just lay there, flattened by the cloud-heavy sky. He could have rolled into the blue ice, been dead in seconds. He chose torture, because his heart wanted it, because it was warm.

Currents brought the captain close and Esa reached for him and lashed the rafts together with a strip of cloth torn from his shirt. "Captain," he said.

"I am no longer."

"You survived. We have to call you something."

"Halvar," said the captain. "But I won't last." His split lips bled.

Nothing propelled that small craft. Not wind, not waves, not hope. The three men had no wishes for themselves. They lacked the strength to drown themselves, and the strength to break off a lose slat and begin to paddle. They did not have enough blood in their hearts to be hungry, or tired or sleepy or dead or alive. They were three thick trunks, cut down.

Esa had not reached into the frozen murk because he had no love to save. He would not have believed lonelier was possible. He rested his head on the wood and smelled its tree-bloody resin.

NOT DYING was the surprise. Washed up on a beach white with crystallized salt, the three men continued to lie still, feeling waves below them that were not there. They half slept, half breathed, half lived. It was a hawk that woke Esa, the shrill call she made before diving, soaring back up with a gray rabbit, legs still running in the air. Esa found his feet, stood dizzy on the earth, trying not to throw up, trying not to fall down. No fires, no people, no dogs or horses. Granite mountains jagged behind them and the shore was a white plain. Shrubs and trees scratched upward. The salt water melted a dark border of pebbled sand between what was frozen and what was liquid.

Ice groaned beneath the weight of the sky. The three men were held there, between upper gods and lower.

HALVAR TOOK Paer's dead arm off with a sharp rock. Esa had a needle in the satchel that he wore, always, around his body. It was an inelegant wound, bound with three of Esa's long hairs, braided together. They expected the arm to infect and green, to kill the body to which it belonged, but each day, it healed more. The scar hardened into a ropy tangle. They built a hut out of snow and carved benches on which to sit and sleep. It held the body heat, what body heat there was. In the spring, once the snow had melted, they planned to build a longhouse into a hillside using rocks and mud and logs. The sun would stop setting and any living thing would hurry to grow as much as it could before the light left. Even the roof of the longhouse would green over with unripe grass.

Paer discovered a whale carcass down the beach and set to work on it, building rib from rib with driftwood, turning the skeleton of the deep-swimmer into the skeleton of a surface-floater. He was not bothered by the slowness of his progress, his one arm sore and tired. He had time, all of time, and where he would sail, even he did not know. Back to the middle, back to his sunken wife?

Halvar's lips healed into an ugly scowl. He began to tunnel, to dig himself down into the ice and snow. He made a maze, as if no kind of lost was lost enough.

And Esa? Esa needed no task to remind him that he would die alone. He sat at the top of the bluff, watching the horizon for anything at all.

SURVIVAL OF BODY was not the question for the three lost men, not yet anyway. There were fish in the sea, reindeer to be hunted, washed-up branches to be sharpened into spears. There was snow that could be melted and drunk. The three men ate their breakfast together around the fire pit, in their world of lost ice. They took turns boiling the dried meat until it softened and they could chew it. It felt like nutrition but not like food. They let the meat-steam fog their faces like some warm, wet heaven. They thought of honey, finger-scooped and glistening. They remembered summer, bushes swollen with berries. They remembered the black-red rot on the ground, thick with flies. The men would have eaten that now, greedily.

Esa wanted to say "Good morning," but he didn't, because morning meant afternoon and afternoon meant evening, and he could not think of another night. The other two stooped their shoulders over their bowls and drank the hot-watery broth. After, Halvar went out to his trenches, to deepen. Paer went out to his boat and chiseled away at the rot. Esa left the snow hut, left the last of the fire and went to sit on top of the bluff where he watched the horizon until it scrambled before him, until water and sky flipped, became borderless. He lay down on his back and closed his eyes. Even his dreams were of blank blue expanses, cold against cold.

ESA SMELLED HER FIRST. Fishy and rotted, the slog of deep water. He thought: *Great, whales washing up dead all over.* You can't move a dead whale; you have to let it rot, you have to live in its rot until it is finished. A year can pass before the skeleton appears, that great bowl of bones. Esa, before he had even opened his eyes, imagined this time next year, crawling into the empty carcass, hoping to drift away.

There was no whale. The beach was empty of sea-giants. Something flicked, a big fish, close to the water. It was in the approach that Esa saw greeny hair at the top. It was when he got close that he saw a face. "Oh," he said, because what do you say when a mermaid washes up? She looked unwell. She looked possibly dead. Esa knelt a few feet away, trying to calculate the danger. She could bite, or sting, or enchant. She could drag him off to sea. He let the small waves joggle her body, but when she loosened from the sand and seemed like she might drift back out, Esa drew close and grabbed her by the tail. Her scales were dim. She did not fight his grasp, but he could see a very faint rise and fall in her chest.

It hardly seemed fair to discover magic, only for the magic to be snuffed out. "I could have used the full miracle," Esa whispered to the mer. She really did smell of the depths. It was an exhausting smell. Esa felt dizzy and unprepared, but he made a soft place in the snow for the newcomer, rolled her into it. Should she be warm or should she be cold? Should she be wet or dry? He took his fur coat off and draped it over her, because this was a woman, though legless and possibly lifeless, and she was the first woman in months. It's good to be a man when there's a woman around.

Esa poured a thin rope of water from his canteen up the mer's body. Tail, belly, chest, throat, chin, nose, forehead. Her skin was pale green, swampy. Esa had to touch her. She was cold and rough. She made his fingertips hum.

Water dripped into her eyes and she flickered. Esa stepped back but she was asleep again, or dead again, or deep in some other depths.

Esa decided the mer should be wetter. He dragged boulders down and made a small pool in the shallows so the woman could not drift away. It was hard work, and he sweated inside his leathers, had to sit down and rest. Esa drank all his water, but he was still thirsty so he chipped pieces of ice into his canteen and held it close to his body until solid turned to liquid. The reward: for fifty paces, he hugged the thick, fishy body to himself, felt the scaly slap of the tail, the reedy riches of her hair. "Let's get away from here," he heard himself say. "Take me to your fathoms." When he laid her down, he fell in, too, and though the water was just this side of unfrozen, he stayed there, floating, his breath gone, his mind cold-quiet, his insides swimming. Esa smelled the mer's neck, felt a gentle pulse. She was a little bit alive. Any kind of alive was enough.

Esa, at night, let the steam steam his face. Tried to act like it was a day like every single other. Halvar said, "What was it like to be warm?"

"I can't remember," said Paer. But Esa remembered because there was a new ember in him. One white coal.

Esa remembered being a child, waiting for his parents to emerge from their bed. He knelt on the floor, jealous that his mother and father were alone together, jealous enough that he lifted the heavy skin and walked into the sweat-muggy room. His father stood up, shaggy and huge, picked Esa up by the hair and threw him out into the snow. From something that warm to something that cold. That is how Esa had always thought of love: a shock to the skin.

IN THE MORNING, Paer was out when the others got up. Esa felt an itch to run and check on his mer, but he tried to stay even. Halvar grunted and scratched his big chest, stretched to find his feet. "Trenches today?" Esa asked, which was a stupid question because it was trenches every day for Halvar. Trenches were the whole of his existence. He kept himself buried in a long maze, big enough to fill with a thousand men and elaborate enough to keep those men alive through a great siege. The trenches wound like the fingers of a river delta all around camp, separating, connecting, pooling in strategically placed restocking areas where Halvar had carved shelves into the snow and ice. They were deep enough to hide an average-sized man, though Halvar's head stuck out as he worked so that Esa could track him, the floating head making its way through the labyrinth, disappearing to dig. For a moment, no Halvar, and then a shovelful of snow sprayed out, glittered in the sunlight.

PAER GOT UP in the night, sleepless and wretched. The world glowed with discontent. Emptiness was everywhere. There was mist over the water, a hover of wetter air. The horizon was dark purple—weather was on its way. Paer thought about boiling snow to drink, or trying to get less hungry somehow. He did not bother to think about heat. Way down below on the beach he saw a big fish, moonlit, even from a distance. Shimmering. Paer felt his blood change direction, his slack heartbeat tighten. He began to make his way through the stiffened snow, picking his steps carefully. With one arm, balance was different and slipping was bad. Paer was slow and careful, trying to keep his dumb body from further harm. He thought he heard an animal, something hoofed, something with putrid breath and ice in its beard, but when he stopped, so did the sound. He realized that he had heard an animal. The scavenging beast hoofing at the ice was Paer.

He slid the last few feet down to the rocky shore, and the fish came into focus, but it was not a fish, not completely. She was also a woman, and immediately his eyes made a wife of her, made her familiar, made her his long-lost. Paer collapsed over her, rolled her into his arm, let the waterlogged mass of her soak his clothes. "You found your way," he said. He felt her shallow breaths on his neck, and Paer wept.

IT WAS AFTERNOON when Halvar put his head out of the tunnel because the sun had grown suddenly bright. It had been a long time since he needed to squint. It was not warm, but it could have been, and he let his mind be tricked. He felt the sun find his face, settle over him. He felt a strange cheer come. Maybe he was a better man than he had thought or the gods were worse. Maybe in this world he was considered good. He thought of the shipboard kiss, his milky daughter, her dead, him alive. He considered sacrificing something, offering his thanks, but there was no reason to draw attention. If the gods wanted to hear their praises, they could come inside his head.

Halvar looked out at the old sea, the horrible, patient sea. At the shore, he saw something glint. A fish, he thought. Dinner. Anything other than dried meat. Halvar had not run in so long, but his legs seemed to remember. Heat spread through his lungs, which were big dry caves inside him. He almost yelled, "Fish!" but stopped himself. He did not have to share, there was no rule that said any of this treasure belonged to those who did not find it.

And what treasure. He saw his daughter, salt-eaten and aged. *Stupid girl,* he thought, *to think you could escape me, escape my love.* She was helpless and fleshy and alive enough to take. Not dinner, but another way to feed. Halvar kept himself from thinking, knowing his mind could easily unmake this reward. Either he deserved her or he did not. Halvar took off leather and wool and his skin below was white and pruned from being covered so long. He smelled like a dog's kill, buried and dug up later. He stood naked over the maid, dragged her onto the beach and lay down on top of her, her two breasts in his hands, wrung out. "The whole ship went down for you."

The maid turned her head away and Halvar saw a smile slip across her face.

The maid opened her eyes and looked at him. And then she twisted, and the scales on her tail sliced him from belly to ankle. Hundreds of tiny knives, across his sweat-softened skin.

The maid rolled herself back down to the water and left Halvar, blood-patterned, tortured by his own stripes.

ESA HAD WAITED for a salve to spread on the everyday wounds, those scrapes on his heartskin from being alive and from wanting. On that big ship, surrounded by marrieds, he had hoped for an alone-with-me person. Two and no more. He had imagined cupping the girl's face in his hands, feeling the bones beneath, knowing the shape so well he would have recognized even her sun-dried skeleton, a thousand years later. Esa thought a love like that deserved its own lands, a brighter tundra. When he was young, he had begun to gather gifts for his beloved. Whalebone coins and reindeer combs, necklaces with locks of horse-mane at the end. Esa put a ring around his ankle, promising before anyone had asked him to. Its twin was sewn into his undershirt, circling his heart like a target.

Esa thought of going to visit his mer, but he had to think this out first. He wanted to ask for her forever. He wanted to tell her that he felt her scales in his bloodstream, that he was swum full of her. It began to snow. Esa dragged a piece of cloth outside and sat on it, his back against a pine, watching the sky fill with flakes. The mer was ankleless, so Esa planned to click the ring around her wrist. He kept saying, "I know it always happens this way, a wrecked sailor, a mermaid. How do I make you believe me?" Even in his mind, she knew better.

THE MER WAS OLD, hundreds of years of swimming behind her. Love worked differently in that kind of time. More chances to lose something and more chances to gain it back. Her loves had been in the thousands. Red-haired ships' captains, boys just old enough to want to use their bodies, whales, others of her own kind. She was too tired now, too worn through to love anyone back. But here she was, a little alive still, and why not let her good body go to use. Why not let her skin and scales mean something miraculous to these lost boys, the poor land-bound humans, outposted at the shore between one nothing and another.

The clouds came apart. Snow and snow and snow and the earth was gone. It fell silent and heavy. A new, white sea was born. The snow melted when it hit the water but it covered the mer. She was whitened, only strong enough to clean her face. This storm might finally be the thing to bury her.

ESA STOOD ON high ground and searched for Halvar in the tunnels. He thought about going in, turning the turns of Halvar's high-walled maze, but the sky did not look like it would clear by nightfall, and Esa imagined the whiteness and the darkness, and he knew that he would not find his way out again. Halvar, he hoped, had some dried meat in his leathers. Halvar, he hoped, had made a den in the ice for burrowing. Esa thought of the big man lying still, trying to keep his own heat.

PAER SQUATTED AT THE FIRE, keeping it alive a moment longer. The wood was wet and whiny. He would bring broth to his finned wife, and when she was warm and ready, he would drag her down to the water's edge. He had considered dragging her across the white earth to his whaleship where they could live, tending and waiting until they died weeks or months or years from now.

He could have dragged her, but he would not. His love was not a carcass. She had grown a tail to be with him again, and now it was his turn. Paer would remove his animal skins until only his own pink leather remained, and he would wade into the water, which would burn him with cold, and he would tie one end of a rope around each of their waists and one-arm swim her, slowly, through the ice-thick sea. He would fight for air, and he knew that his heart would pound for dry land and dry cloth, but if he would keep swimming, if he stayed submerged, his legs would begin to freeze. Paer did not know how the next steps went, how a man turned into a fish. Yet knowing rarely made the journey easier. It was up to the gods now. Man and wife would swim for a long time and turn over onto their backs when the swimming became too difficult, and the snow falling on their faces would feel soft and warm and generous, the sky offering itself to them, both legless now, waiting for the leagues to take them home.

HALVAR, BLEEDING, could not make himself move. He could not forgive the trillions of white-hot flakes or the pink-black sky or the sound of the sea or his own body, reckless and stupidly alive. He should have gone down with his ship. He should have been more ferocious, or less. He stopped wiping the snow from his face. The snow dressed his wounds, covered his weeping skin. Halvar could hear the thrum of his heart change. He lost his edges first: toes and fingers. By nightfall, he was a small white hill, no bigger than any other drift. His body would not matter again until snowmelt, when a pair of bears, sleepish and starving, came to dig around his skeleton for mushrooms sprouted from the richer soil.

ESA WENT to his mer. He would stay all night, brush the snow off. He worried that she was cold, though he knew the deep water must be just as chilly. He said, "I can't live in water and you can't live on land, but we can stay here at the edges. I'll build a house on stilts, over the sea with a hole in the floor and a ladder. The place where air and water meet—that's our home together." *Sometimes it takes a shipwreck,* he thought. *Sometimes it takes a tragedy.* The mer washed back and forth with the waves. She looked into Esa's puddle-brown eyes. It was good, a service, to let someone believe.

"I was worried about the same thing." Paer was standing above them, holding a broom he had made from pine needles. He knelt down to kiss her. "She found me," he said. He brushed his hand over her frozen hair.

Esa knew that this was not Paer's wife. This love was his love. He imagined wrestling Paer to the water, holding his head under. The snow would still be falling when he was done. He looked at the man beside him brushing their sea-beauty with gathered needles. How tended-to the mer looked. She smiled up at the boys. Esa was heartswollen. It would be a service to let Paer believe. Maybe, he thought, they would all set off in Paer's boat, the mer trailing behind at the end of a long rope handspun from their hair. The snow would eventually stop and the black sky would grow delirious with stars. They would sail to her kingdom and some of them would survive, or none of them would.

Esa had enough blood to love the mer but not enough to be the only one. He wanted to kiss her but Paer was already there, his beard frozen and his mouth warm. Esa was freezing, every living thing was, and the world had slowed down so much that Esa was not sure it moved at all. The water had turned to ice, stopped lapping. The air was hardly breathable. Time had quit on them. Esa lay down in the snow and put his head on the mer's belly. Her skin had no discernible temperature. Esa felt Paer's glove on his hair. His father? Home had found him, he thought.

Acknowledgments

All the thanks in the world to:

Sarah McGrath, Katie Freeman, Claire McGinnis, Jynne Martin, Geoff Kloske, Kate Stark, Danya Kukafka, Lindsay Means, Helen Yentus, Grace Han and every single person at Riverhead: it's a little bit absurd how brilliant this team is.

PJ Mark, Ian Bonaparte and Marya Spence.

The editors and journals where these stories first appeared: Cressida Leyshon & *The New Yorker*; Lorin Stein & *The Paris Review Daily*; Michelle Wildgen & *Tin House*; Lauren Groff & *Ploughshares*; Jamie Quatro & *Oxford American*; Nick Haramis & *Bullett*.

Matt Sumell, Michael Andreason and Marisa Matarazzo, who often saw these stories before anyone else.

Michelle Latiolais, Ron Carlson and Christine Schutt: still not done thanking you and never will be.

My ever-supportive family and friends.

©Teo Grossman

Ramona Ausubel has long been revered as a master of magical and imaginative fiction. Originally from Santa Fe, New Mexico, and now residing in California, she is the winner of the PEN Center USA Literary Award for Fiction and the VCU Cabell First Novelist Award, and was a finalist for the New York Public Library Young Lions Fiction Award. From her first novel, *No One Is Here Except All of Us* (called "fantastical and ambitious" by *The New York Times Book Review*) to her short story collection *A Guide to Being Born* (which Aimee Bender called "fresh, delicate, beautiful, expressive, otherworldly") to the acclaimed novel *Sons and Daughters of Ease and Plenty* (heralded by *The New York Times* as "weird and wonderful"), Ramona Ausubel immerses her readers in worlds that are at once powerfully recognizable and wildly imaginative, offering us a rich, new way of seeing while also captivating us with her sparkling storytelling. Her fiction has become an important piece of the landscape of American fiction.

The debut novel by Ramona Ausubel about a village that tries to save itself through sheer force of imagination.

In 1939, the residents of a tiny Romanian village are counting on their isolation to protect them from the catastrophe sweeping Europe. When a mysterious stranger is washed up on the riverbank and the illusion of peace is shattered, the villagers are forced to acknowledge the precariousness of their situation. At the suggestion of an eleven-year-old girl and the washed up stranger, the villagers decide they will reinvent the world.

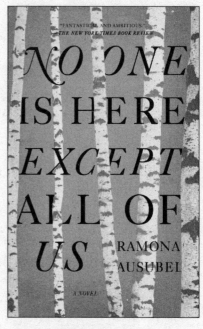

In rich, luminous, sure-footed prose, Ramona Ausubel has created a hugely ambitious story about the bigness of being alive as an individual, as a member of a tribe, and as a participant in history. *No One Is Here Except All of Us* explores how we use storytelling to survive and to shape our own truths.

"Fantastical and ambitious."

—*The New York Times Book Review*

An enthralling collection that uses the world of the imagination to explore the heart of the human condition.

In each of her eleven stories, Ramona Ausubel uses her inimitable style, her fantastical ambition, and her gift for the imaginative to expose the fundamentals of the human condition as she charts the cycle of love from conception to gestation to birth.

A pregnant teenage girl believes she will give birth to any number of strange animals rather than a

human baby; an expectant father wakes to find that small drawers have appeared in the center of his chest; a girl discovers the ghost of a Civil War hero living in the woods behind her house. These stories are about the moments when we pass from one part of life into another, about the love that finds us in the dark and pulls us, finally, through.

"Aggressively imaginative." —*The New York Times*

An imaginative novel from an award-winning author about a wealthy New England family in the 1960s and '70s that suddenly loses its fortune—and its bearings.

Labor Day 1976, Martha's Vineyard. Summering at the family beach house along this moneyed coast of New England, Fern and Edgar—married with three children—are happily preparing for a family birthday celebration when they learn that the unimaginable has occurred: there is no more money.

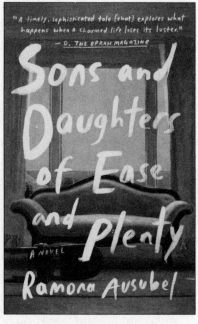

Brimming with humanity and wisdom, humor and bite, and imbued with both the whimsical and the profound, *Sons and Daughters of Ease and Plenty* is a story of American wealth, class, family, and mobility, approached by Ramona Ausubel with a breadth of imagination and understanding that is fresh, surprising, and exciting.

"Weird and wonderful." **—*The New York Times***

"A timely, sophisticated tale [that] explores what happens when a charmed life loses its luster."

—*O, The Oprah Magazine*